# DECEIVED BY HOOD LOVE 2

## CHEY

*Chapter One*

# JERVON

Ten minutes ago, I was catching a few hours of sleep next to Shawnda until it was time for me to get up and return home with Fayth, when the loud banging along with the ringing of the doorbell jolted me and Shawnda awake. Automatically, our minds went to it being nobody but her deranged soon to be ex-husband, yet again here to beg and plead for her to reconsider their divorce. But never in a million years did I think the person waking us up would be Fayth, so coming down the stairs and seeing her standing there hurt, broke me to pieces.

Now here I am running up the street, trying to get to her, silently praying she wasn't dead. The closer I got to the mangled two-door Honda and seeing it folded in half, the faster my heart pounded. I could hear the driver of the trash truck asking Fayth if she was OK and letting her know that help was on the way.

When my eyes landed on the love of my life, I froze in place. Blood was pouring from her head, but she was alive. I wanted to curse at the dumb ass driver because he was applying pressure to her wound with his shirt he had now taken off. Granted, that was the logical thing to do, but not when the piece of material was dirty and full of bacteria.

"Fayth, baby, remain still, OK? I'm right here! Can you tell me what if anything hurts? Can you feel your legs?" I rattled off question after question without giving her an opportunity to answer one.

When I went to reach in and touch her, she screamed, "Don't fucking touch me!"

Although it was clear she was in a world of pain from the wreck, I knew that what was hurting her more was her heart I had broken. The fact Fayth was pushing me away and allowing the germ-infested trash man render aid until help arrived, knowing the risks involved, only exemplified just how much she hated me in the moment.

"Fayth, I understand you're mad, but let me help you until first responders get here. I'm a doctor, dammit," I begged. I could tell her legs were pinned in the metal, so pulling her from the car was impossible. "Sir, can you move out of my way? I'm a doctor. And please call and see where the hell these people are at."

"I don't want you near me right now. Go worry about your pregnant bitch, and get away from me."

I could finally hear sirens and was relieved because this big muthafucka still was applying pressure, listening to Fayth by not allowing me to take over. His dumb ass knew how to empty people's garbage into his truck and not how to safely help someone who had injuries. "I understand you're mad, but you're not using your head. At least take that damn dirty ass shirt off your head."

What I just said must have finally registered in her head because she told the man to grab the sweater she kept in her back seat and use that instead. Fayth was anemic and often, even during the summer when it was hot as hell outside, she would be chilly, so she always had something in the car to put on to keep her warm.

The paramedics were the first to pull up, and seconds later, the fire department. They had to utilize the Hurst jaws of life tool to cut Fayth free from the vehicle. But first, they bandaged her head, and the second they removed her, she screamed out in agonizing pain. I knew from the shrill that Fayth suffered broken legs, and it was all my fault. I couldn't help myself as I started to bark out orders to the EMTs. They placed a neck brace and two leg braces on her while she laid on the stretcher.

While pushing her toward the back of the ambulance, I yelled out, "I'll be right behind you, baby." It sounded like she told me not to bother, but I wasn't sure.

When I got back to Shawnda's house, I found her sitting in the chair with her legs crossed, looking amused. That was when I realized I was outside the whole time in nothing but my boxers and sock. "So, are you going to tell me what all that was about?"

I really didn't have time to have this conversation with her ass, seeing as the real woman I wanted to be with was on her way to the emergency room. "Not right now, Shawnda. I have to get to the hospital."

"No, what you need to do is sit the hell down and tell me something, and you better hope it's good," she replied sternly.

"I'll come back later and answer whatever questions you have then, but right now, I have somewhere to be, and that's more important."

I was grateful she didn't dispute or hold me up but instead watched me go upstairs to put on my pants and grab my things. While looking for my shirt was when it dawned on me that Shawnda had it on. "Aye, can you bring me my shirt?" I yelled down the stairs while I went to the bathroom to brush my teeth.

Seeing that Shawnda hadn't moved, I went back in the room, went in her dresser drawer, and grabbed something for her to change into. Going back downstairs, I went back into the front room that, up until this evening, she was against anyone sitting down in, and handed her what I had for her to put on. She looked at me like I had eight heads.

"Look, I don't have time for this right now, Shawnda. I have to go."

"Does it look like I'm stopping you?"

Taking a deep breath to calm myself down and pinching the bridge of my nose, I counted to five and asked as politely as I could, given the situation, "Can you please take off my shirt so I can leave?"

"No."

"Why are you doing this? Why are you making this so damn hard?"

"I'm not doing anything, Jervon. I asked you a question when you came inside, and you decided that you will answer it on your time. I'm only following your lead and playing your game. Therefore, I'll take off this shirt and hand it to you when I'm good and damn ready to, or, you can leave without it. It's up to you."

Realizing that there was no way getting around this conversation, I figured I may as well answer her questions and keep them short and simple so I could get the hell on and be by Fayth's side. The longer I took, the more deeper I was digging my grave, and if I wanted for her to hear me out, then I had to get to the hospital. One thing about Fayth that wasn't really a good quality was the way she let her thoughts get in the way, and once her mind thought it had something figured out, there was no changing it.

"Look, me and Fayth have been together going on six years and engaged just about five. We've been having some differences, and that's when you and I met. She's a good girl, and me walking away from her wasn't a good move with how fragile she's been, so I chose to play along with us getting married. She don't have no family or friends, and right now, she's banged up and needs me. I'm going to the hospital to make sure everything is OK, and I'll be back here later."

I was lying my ass off, but I needed Shawnda, and keeping her content was just as important as making sure Fayth didn't leave me. I needed them both but for different reasons; however, I only really wanted one of them, and right now, she was lying in a hospital bed.

"And the award for best supporting actor goes to," Shawnda said, clapping her hands, but she could've kept all those dramatics to her damn self.

"You know what, I'll stop and grab a tee from the twenty-four-hour Walmart. I'll get up with you when I feel like you ready to be an adult about shit." Without another word uttered between the two of us, I left out the house and looked in my trunk to see if I had something in there to put on. Luckily for me, I had some old uniforms from when I worked at the hospital that I never dropped off. Grabbing a top, I slipped it over my head and got in my car. As I started the engine, I looked up and saw Shawnda at the door, watching my every move. I couldn't make out her facial expression, but right now, her feelings had to be put on pause while I tended to Fayth's.

Arriving to the hospital, I practically broke the Guinness World Record running into the building to see about Fayth. "Hi, my fiancée was brought in by ambulance about forty minutes ago. She was involved in a car accident. Her name is Fayth..."

I didn't even get to give her last name when the woman at the front desk, that must be new because she didn't recognize me, said, "Marshall, and I'm taking it that you're Dr. Jervon Collins?"

"I am. Could you please direct me to where she is being seen?" I said, ready to walk toward the doors while she let me in.

"I'm afraid I can't do that, Dr. Collins. Miss Marshall gave strict orders upon arrival pertaining to any visitors. She doesn't want to be bothered. Is there anything else I can assist you with?"

I wanted to cuss this lady out and demand that she let me in, but seeing as I knew hospital policies and that on the other side of the double doors were at least two security officers, I wasn't going to chance being kicked out the place. "Yes, can you have whoever is treating her come to the waiting room and let me know what's going on with her?"

Looking at me without an ounce of sympathy, she shook her head and informed me that Fayth also signed a nondisclosure form where her information couldn't be shared without her consent. I understood she was upset, but she was really going too far. There was no need for her to shut me out the way she was. In the past, I had gotten places by using my good looks and charm, so I decided to try and see where it got me this time.

"Kelly," I said, reading her name from the hospital issued lanyard clipped onto her shirt, "my fiancée suffered a pretty serious bang to her head, and I'm almost certain under any other circumstances, she would never have put those restrictions in place. It's clear that Fayth's injuries are prohibiting her from making sound decisions, which is all the more reason why I must be back there to ensure she knows what she is doing."

I closed off my mini speech with a smile but noticed Kelly's face remained the same. "You can save all that for someone else who hasn't heard about your womanizing ways, Dr. Collins. I might have bought that had your fiancée not have left here earlier in the night looking for you. Someone who she had no clue no longer worked in this facility because he has been accused of sexual harassment of his co-workers. Now if you don't mind, there is somebody standing behind you looking for information on their loved one, and I have a job to do."

Hearing that Fayth also learned about the false allegations against me made everything ten times worse than they already were. I needed to think and think fast on how I was going to get out of all this mess and still have my woman, because losing Fayth was not an option. Feeling defeated, I slammed my hands on the desk before putting them up to express I didn't mean it. I turned around and walked back out the door and to my car.

Not wanting to return to Shawnda's house, I headed to the house I shared with Fayth. Being alone would give me the time I needed to gather my thoughts and come up with a game plan on how to win my woman back. Living without Fayth in my life was not an option. The only reason for me even carrying on with Shawnda to begin with was to try and keep up with the lifestyle me and Fayth started living together. Shawnda was providing me with product that I was able to have Stefon sell. Granted, I'd been mismanaging the money and not putting it into the joint account like I should have, but that was because Diamonds had become an obsession, and I spent all my money on the dancers.

## Chapter Two

# STEFON

"Aye, I need a big favor from you," Jervon said the second I answered his fifth call in a row. It was late as hell, and I had knocked out with Lenny's little ass. Trinity was still at the club and would be coming in the door any second.

"And what might that be?"

"Go up to the hospital and see if they let you see Fayth."

I knew this man did not just ask me to check on his bitch as if he had was handicap. "Why can't you? I got my son, and my girl ain't home yet."

"Because she ain't fucking with me. And why you still let Trinity dance at that club?" he questioned me.

See, this was exactly why I wanted her ass to quit. It was a bad look on my behalf, like I was cool with her swinging from poles and shit. The last thing I needed was this muthafucka to start judging me like I wasn't a real man because of the line of work my girl was in. I'd been trying to get her to leave, but for some reason, she loved that place.

"I don't know 'bout your relationship, but over here, it's an equal opportunity environment. I don't tell my girl what she can or can't do. If she wants to go swing from poles, vines, or rooftops, then I'm going to support her as long as she comes home to me at night and keeps it real." I was blowing a whole lot of smoke out my ass, but Jervon didn't need to know that.

Jervon chuckled as if he doubted any of what I was saying but I couldn't care less what his square ass thought. "Listen, Fayth got in a pretty bad accident, and the hospital they transported her to is the same one we bumped into each other at. I'm not allowed in the facility, so I have no idea how she's doing. Can you please just go up there, or ask Trinity to stop on her way home from work? I'm going crazy." He begged.

"Get off my line and let me see where Trin at right now. I ain't making no promises tho'." That was all it took for his lame ass to disconnect our call. Before I attempted to call Trin, I wanted to move my little man to his bed. I was thankful Jervon had called because Trin hated when I let Lenny go to bed in our room and not in his own. But that was my G, and I couldn't help it. I missed so much time with him that disciplining him was impossible, and he knew that shit too.

As I was creeping out of his room, Trinity walked in the front door. "Stefon, you better had been checking on Len and not just moved him."

"No, he wasn't asleep in our bed. I just got up when Jervon called me and took a piss. I was heading back to the room to call you when I peeked in and noticed he had kicked his blanket off him. I was trying to catch you before you came in. I guess Jervon's wife was in a wreck, and he wanted to see if you would check in on her."

"Nope." Trinity replied without even considering it, which took me by surprise. Judging from the night we all went out, she appeared to really have liked Fayth, and I would assume she would want to make sure she was okay.

"And why not?" I inquired out of curiosity.

"Because I already know she is okay. She texted me and figured his desperate ass would try to get information from you or me. Did you know he was living a whole nother life with some other woman?" Trinity asked.

Truth be told, I didn't know much about his ass outside of him being a doctor. I didn't believe him when we first met. He was leaving the hospital madder than a muthafucka and bumped into me. We started to exchange words, but then he quickly asked if I knew where to sell any pills. That was music to my ears because I had just arrived back in Boston and was trying to figure out my next move. We went to some little hole in the wall bar to get a feel for one another, and that was when I reached out to Rodney.

Rodney was a known enemy of Montez, and it was no secret. I was taking a big risk by reaching out because, at one point in time, any enemy of Montez was one of mine, but I had a little bit of assistance in making the connection to

Rodney as peaceful as possible. I was ducked off with his sister the whole ten months I was in hiding. She moved away from Boston when things were at their worst, and both Montez and Rodney were losing souljahs left and right. Ronnie didn't want to be caught in the crossfire, so she packed her two kids and left. We were always cool since middle school, so when I found Montez and Trinity in bed and needed to get away, I hit her up.

"Trin, all I know 'bout him is he has a connect to get us product at no damn cost right now. That's unheard of, and I'm taking advantage of it," I told her.

"And that doesn't worry you? Who the hell gets work without paying? What if he ain't a doctor after all and really is with the feds, and they're investigating you and Montez? Have you ever seen him at work?" Trinity rattled off question after question, and they were all good, but I didn't have an answer to nan one of them.

The ringing of my phone grabbed both of our attention, and I knew it wasn't anyone but Jervon. Walking back to the room with my girl on my heels, I picked it up. "Any word?"

"Nah. Trin tried to go up there, but they saying they don't have no patient by the name of Fayth or any car accident victims in the system. Perhaps she's been released already," I suggested.

"I'm at the house, and she isn't here. Can I please talk to Trinity?" he asked. I had the phone on speaker, so there was no need for me to pass it over to her.

"I'm here." Trinity spoke up.

"Can you call Fayth. I need to find my baby."

"Listen, it's not my business, but maybe she wants to be alone and not bothered by you right now. What you did was fucked up. I'll never preach about cheating because I ain't no saint, but you out here living a whole double life with another woman," Trinity blurted out, instantly covering her mouth. Jervon knew I didn't know nothing about his personal life outside of what he had shared with me, and he never told me about any other female but Fayth, so there was no way for Trinity to know any of what she just revealed without Fayth being the person who told her.

"So, you did speak with her? Is she okay?" Jervon questioned, catching on to what Trinity had revealed.

"She sounded hurt but not from the accident. Just give her the space she so clearly needs."

"But where is she? I'm at our house now, and she's not here. I have to find her." Jervon rambled.

Shaking her head, I knew exactly what was coming next from my girl, "She's not there because she doesn't want to be near you. Why are you men so god damn hardheaded and stupid? You know, I used to pray at night for a man like you, Jervon, when you first started coming to Diamonds. You were someone who I thought had it all and could provide the perfect, safe life for me and my son, but boy was I wrong. You're the worst of the worst and living a big ass lie."

I knew I didn't hear this bitch just say she used to fantasize about my new business partner. Fucking my old one wasn't enough! Now she was plotting and planning on moving on to the next one, and here I was going against the grain and getting ready to really make shit legit between us and put a ring on her hoe ass finger. Trinity's disloyal ass would probably beat another muthafucka's meat with the hand I put that shit on.

She must've noticed me tense up because she told Jervon we had to go and hung up before trying to make her way over to where I was standing. "Don't take what I said wrong, Stefon. You left me alone, remember, and those thoughts were before you came back." I heard what she said, but I wasn't listening.

"I'm gonna ask you this one time and one time only. Did you fuck Jervon?" I questioned Trinity while staring her straight in the eye, praying I didn't see any sign of her lying.

"You know what, I'm not even answering that stupid ass question that I already answered the night I fucking realized he was who you were in cahoots with. Fayth already beat you to that. Now you can either believe it or not. That's all up to you," she replied.

Anytime a person avoided giving a straight and direct answer meant they had something to hide, and if Trinity wasn't going to be the one to tell me what I rightfully needed to know, then I knew one of two people who would love to disclose that information. And I damn sure wasn't turning to Jervon, expecting some truth. It appeared his ass was living a whole ass lie out here with more secrets than a teenage girl's diary. The one person who would enjoy telling me all of what I needed to know was Montez.

"It's late. I'm going to sleep," I told Trinity before climbing back into the same spot I was comfortable in not even an hour ago.

"That's not fair. Can you please just talk to me, Stefon. I know what you're thinking, and you wrong."

Chuckling, I said, "You don't know shit, Trin. Just leave it alone, okay, and go wash up for bed. It doesn't even fucking matter. I can't go back in time and change what happened, and neither can you. I just know that any business partners I may gain in the future, I need to keep them from around you."

"Fuck you!" Trinity reacted.

"Nah. I think I'll fuck myself, baby. I'm gonna go look for my own place tomorrow, and we can co-parent when it comes to Lenny. I'll still watch him while you sell pussy."

"Just like that, you gonna give up? That's your damn problem, Stefon. You're a quitter and never fight for what you want. Always quick to run the hell away when shit don't go how you want, or you think you know what the fuck is going on. But seeing as you wanna walk the hell out, get the fuck out my bed and go sleep on the couch." Trinity screeched and then turned away at the doorway. "For the record, dumb ass, no I never fucked Jervon, but maybe I should. It appears we both single now."

It was too late, and the last thing I wanted right now was to have a screaming match with Trinity while my son was asleep. He was just now getting comfortable with me, and I didn't want him to start back being afraid of me. So, I sucked up what she had just said and took my stubborn ass right to the living room and got as comfy as I could on the sofa.

The more I tossed and turned, the more aggravated I got. What I really wanted to do was get the fuck up and storm in the bedroom and fuck Trinity so damn good it reminded her why she would always belong to me. But my pride was keeping me grounded in place as if I had cinderblocks for feet. I was mad at everyone but myself, but truthfully, I was a major player in all this. Had I not left Trinity alone and left her room to lust after other men, then none of this would be happening. Then again, nobody told her to fuck Montez.

Finally saying fuck this uncomfortable ass sofa, I got up and took myself to the room. Trinity was knocked out cold, sleeping dead center of the bed with her legs sprawled. I knew her little ass did that shit on purpose, but that was cool. The little corner she wasn't occupying was enough space for me to get a few hours of sleep in. I needed it too, because I had to decide if this relationship was even worth salvaging, or should I do what I threatened and find a spot of my own.

## Chapter Three

# FAYTH

Never in my life had I ever felt so damn alone. I didn't realize until right now, laying in a hospital bed with a broken leg and fifteen stitches across my forehead, that besides Jervon, I was alone in this world. I wished I could reach out to my family, but hearing 'I told you so' wasn't something I wanted to deal with on top of everything else. If you knew where I came from, then you would get it.

Born and raised in Arkansas, I was the product of a disobedient daughter who ran out and got pregnant at a young age from what my grandparents called ghetto trash. When my alleged sperm donor denied even sleeping with my mother and damn sure didn't stick around to find out if I was indeed his, my mother thought she could shop around for someone to play daddy to me. After countless tryouts, she successfully managed to get one man to stick around and take claim to the two of us.

My new dad was known in the streets as one of the city's most dangerous gang members, and one night, when I was about sixteen, he was murdered by someone from his own set. Crazy, ain't it. Not even a rival member took the notorious Trip down. That was when I made a vow to get the hell away from that lifestyle and make something of myself. I buried myself in books and went away to college to make something of my life.

When I met Jervon and brought him home to meet my mom and her new lover, Dro, they told me I was blinded by him, and he wasn't all he made himself out to be. I told them they were crazy, and he was gonna be a doctor. Dro's exact words were, "I know a sneaky muthafucka when I see one, and Jervon has snake written all over him." He claimed any man who couldn't look another straight in the eye while holding a conversation, wasn't to be trusted, and Jervon's eyes wandered more than a hyper child at Chuck E. Cheese. When I asked Jervon why would Dro say that, he told me it was because Dro's facial tattoos scared him.

I was due to be discharged from the hospital in the morning and had no idea where I was going. There was no way I could return to the house I shared with Jervon without having to face him and his infidelity. I still loved him, and the last thing I wanted was to become that weak woman who felt as long as she had a piece of the man, then it was better than having none.

Jervon has been relentless on trying to reach me. Trinity had let me know he had been giving her a headache by stopping by the club every night, three days straight, asking her for my location. She also made it known that he didn't stay and receive dances while there, and it was becoming an issue with her boss. He threatened to fire her behind it because he felt like she had something outside the job going on with Jervon which resulted in him losing money.

Not wanting Trinity to get fired, I decided to try and reach out to Montez. I mean, after allowing him to fuck me all over his office, the same night, my world fell apart. Not wanting this man to get my number, I used my phone to find the number to Diamonds then using the hospital landline phone, I called, and the second the line connected, I froze. It was Montez who answered, and now I was stuck. All I could think about was how he made me feel.

"Stop playing on my fucking line. I can hear you breathing hard, so it's got to be one of you hoes I dicked down," he said.

"Excuse me?" I said. "You might not remember me, but I'm the girl from the gas station."

Just saying that, I felt dumb as fuck. "Damn, baby. You want some more of this dick already?"

I did, but I wasn't going to tell him that, because just admitting it to myself had me feeling dirty. But I also didn't want to make a fool out of myself and just hang up. I had to remember why I even called to begin with. "Actually, I'm calling on behalf of one of your dancers. I got into a wreck the same night we um... well you know... and I've been in the hospital ever since. She has been my eyes and ears where my ex is concerned, and she told me that you've been giving her a hard time because he hasn't been back to spend money in your club. I know I don't have any say in what you do, but don't fire her behind Jervon not spending money anymore. I'm sure he'll be back eventually, once he gets over the fact I'm not going back to him."

"I don't know who you been talking to, because I don't do the read between the lines thing. I'm more direct, so unless you wanna tell me who I'm so called getting rid of, then stop wasting my muthafuckin time."

I couldn't believe how this man just spoke to me. Or perhaps I could. "Trinity. I met her one night my ex took me out to dinner." I left out the part of her with her man who happens to be Jervon's hoodlum partner of some sort. I knew there was some sort of history between Stefon and Montez and really didn't want any parts of it. However, I stood by not wanting Trinity to lose her job.

"You really is naïve, I see. Baby, let me worry about what goes on in my club and what I will allow, and you worry about what goes on around you. I'm not the smartest muthafucka on this planet, but even I can see just having two conversations with you that you ain't too bright."

Not knowing what to say or even how to feel about what Montez just said, I stayed quiet. How was I supposed to know I was engaged to a stranger that I thought I knew? "There you go breathing all heavy in my ear again. Let me find out you over there playing in that wet wet thinking about me."

"No, I was not, and please stop mentioning what happened that night. It was a mistake, even if Jervon deserved me cheating on him. I am the one suffering laying in a hospital bed healing," I stated.

"Let me find out he's a whole bitch out here putting hands on a defenseless woman."

"Oh no. I crashed my car after finding out about him having a baby on the way." Just repeating that shit made me feel dumb all over again. I kept racking my brain, trying to see if I missed the signs that Jervon wasn't being truthful, but I kept coming up empty. There were two different kinds of liars in this world. One that just lied to lie and didn't really put energy or thought into the tales they told. I mean, they would tell you something minor and be lying for no reason. Then you had someone like Jervon who would completely blindside you and have you questioning yourself. His level of lying was the worst. The kind that would leave someone broken.

"Damn, that's a bad hit all the way around, but you ain't exactly loyal. It didn't take me much to convince you that your man ain't shit before I had you bent over my desk screaming for me to fuck you harder."

"Do you have to keep bringing that up? I was caught up in the moment and not thinking straight. Otherwise, it wouldn't have taken place," I told Montez because I didn't want him to think I made it a habit of just sleeping with strangers just because.

"Well, next time you feel like being caught up in the moment, you know where to find me, and I'll gladly assist you, but as far as the reason behind you calling, as long as Trinity does what I told her to do and stops losing focus on other shit, she don't got nothing to worry 'bout. You take care, beautiful," Montez said then disconnected the call.

While we were on the phone, I couldn't wait to hang up, because I was embarrassed by my actions, but now that he had hung up, I wanted to call back just to talk. Now, what we could possibly have to talk about, I wasn't sure, but I realized that brief five minutes had me feeling better than I had been. Looking down at the buzzing phone in my lap and seeing it was Jervon, I knew I had to get this conversation out of the way. There wouldn't be a *perfect* time, so I answered, instantly regretting it.

"Fayth, baby, where are you? Please say something. Are you OK? Let me come see you so we can talk. I can explain. It's not what you're thinking," he rattled off.

"Jervon, I only answered to get this conversation over and done with, but make no mistakes about it. There is absolutely not a damn thing you can say or do to make things right, so whatever lie or story you think you're going to feed me and think I'm gonna be stupid enough to believe you, is a waste of time. I need for you to pack up your shit and move it into your fiancée's by tomorrow so I can go home to my house and rest."

"No, I ain't leaving, and neither are you. We are going to fix this and get things back to how they used to be. I got lost, Fayth, baby, and I fucked up big time. I know that, and I know that it's going to take a lot of work time and effort on my behalf to get you to forgive me. Please give me that chance. I love you, Fayth, and the thing with Shawnda is just business. I don't love her. I don't even know why she told you she's pregnant. She can't have kids, she told me."

Chucking, I replied, "Is that supposed to make me feel better? Whether or not your little soon to be wife that you kept hidden, can have kids, can't have kids, or is just as much as a low down dirty liar like you, doesn't take away from the fact I caught you at another woman's house in your damn boxers when I thought you were at work at a job you were fired from because you were trying to fuck the staff. I know I didn't have the perfect body up until recently, but damn, I at least thought you were satisfied with me and me only."

"That's not how it went, Fayth. Please, let's sit down and talk face to face." Jervon pleaded.

"Are you going to be gone when I get to the house, or do I have to find a room somewhere?" I questioned, not bothering to respond to what he was requesting.

"Fayth..." he started to say, but I cut him off.

"No, Jervon. You don't get to say nothing else other than 'yes, I will be gone' or 'no, go get yourself a room, Fayth!'" I yelled, hanging up on him, no longer wanting to give Jervon another second of my time. It wasn't getting me anywhere but even more stressed.

I was trying my best to remain calm, but the more I thought about how Jervon was downplaying everything, the angrier I was getting. It was like he didn't understand what he had been doing was wrong. The man has not one but two damn fiancées. And to think I originally thought he was having an affair with Trinity when I used to spy on him at the club. Just thinking about all the secrets that I had found out about hads me wondering what else he could be hiding. Whatever it may be, I wasn't trying to stick around and find out. My days of playing Dora The Explorer ended when I met a trash truck the other night.

Feeling the pain starting to increase, I buzzed for the nurse so she could bring in something to take the edge off before it got too bad. "Hello, Ms. Marshall. What can I help you with?" the tiny but friendly girl asked.

"Is it time for my pain medication yet? I'd really like to nip it in the bud before it gets too bad. Also, can you ask the doctor when I can shower. I just don't feel all that clean taking these bird baths, and with me going home tomorrow, I want to make sure I'm able to wash up like a normal person," I said.

Clicking a few things in her computer, she let me know she would be back with something for the pain and would check in with the doctor about showering. I knew I couldn't get the cast that was currently on my leg wet, but there had to be something other than standing over a sink that I could do. "OK, Fayth. I'm going to assist you to the showers down the hall, and once we get back to the room, I'll give you your medication."

"Don't you think it would make more sense to give it to me before the shower if I'm already feeling some pain. By putting it off will only increase it, and then it'll take longer for it to go away. I'm trying to avoid it getting to that point," I suggested.

Nodding, she let me know that where she agreed with me, it was the logical way of seeing things, but the doctor had stated for me to have it after the shower, and she was only following orders. I couldn't be mad at her, and had I not been already feeling drained, I would have requested to speak with the physician directly. "Well, let's get this shower over with. I can't wait to be out of here and in a normal bed," I expressed to nobody specifically.

I was at the club, getting my money, per usual. Tonight was packed, and I had just finished giving a couple a lap dance. I could tell these two were still in their newlywed stage. These were the best folks to give these kinds of dances to, because the women enjoyed it and the men loved it. And in return, I made triple the money. I had a way of painting a picture of a night of fun with the male and female, with just a simple dance, and in return, they blessed me lovely with all their money. The more I grinded on the female, the more cash I felt being stuffed on my garter belt.

"Damn, baby. Let me find out you into pussy!" I overheard the man say to his girl as I strutted away. If she wasn't before, I knew I damn sure gave her room to think about it.

Just as I was heading to freshen up before I took center

stage, Stacks, the head of security, stopped me to let me know that Montez wanted to speak with me in his office. I wasn't in the mood for his shenanigans, and quite frankly, I was beginning to think about quitting this damn job, just to avoid his ass. It was crazy how, just a few months ago, I was so deep in lust—yes, I said lust—with this man, and now he made my skin crawl. "Tell him give me a few minutes. I need to clean up some before it's time for my final set."

Nodding his head to let me know that he would relay the message, Stacks walked toward the back staircase to head up to where Montez's office was located. I went into the locker room and used my Summers Eve wipes to freshen up some before I changed outfits. I took pride in wearing a new set for each time I took the stage. I thought it was tacky and boring when some of these girls thought coming in with their $2.50 Walmart thongs on, it was good enough to perform with. That was what separated me from them. It was also why I made bank and they made pennies in comparison.

The second I entered Montez's office, the smile on my face fell, seeing the look on his face. He had his typical evil ass smile on his face. "I don't appreciate you sending your little chihuahua on me to stick up for you."

Confused about what he could be referring to, I brushed it off like it was nothing. "I don't know what you talking about, crazy fool, but if you don't mind, I'm due up front in about two minutes, and unless you want me to skip out on this money, then I'll take a seat and entertain your theory."

Like I suspected, he waved me off, and I gladly got the fuck from around his ass. I wasn't feeling the energy he was sending no way, and in order for me to perform to my best ability, it was best I remained as relaxed as possible. Another thing most of these girls did wrong was their choice in music to perform to. They tended to play what was trending and slow grind to it. Not me. I was strictly reggae. Mainly Spice. She got my body moving. I got lost in a zone whenever I listened to her music. So much so, I just closed my eyes and pictured myself bouncing my pussy off a nice juicy dick. Whenever I took the stage, all eyes in the building landed on me. That was why I knew no matter what Montez threatened to do, he would never get rid of me. I was a headliner and brought the house down every night.

As soon as they announced me taking the stage and "Back Way" by Vybz Kartel started, the lights dimmed even lower, and I appeared, ready to fuck shit up. I got lost in my zone as I handled the pole like a toy. I slam dunked my ass in the blink of an eye, as I dropped from the top of the pole to the floor, making sure my ass bounced to the beat. I made my rounds around the stage, making sure I divided up the time left equally. I'd been told I had a way of making customers feel like I was putting on a show for their eyes only and left them wanting more.

Many had propositioned me with large sums of money if I would go home with them and give private shows. As good as that sounded, I always declined. Contrary to popular belief, I

was far from a hoe. I knew it appeared that way, seeing as I
cheated on my man with his cousin and then sucked up
Jervon. But outside of them, I'd only been with one other
man, and that wasn't willingly.

The song went off, and I scooped up all my money. And
yes, it was a lot. These folks showed out for me tonight, and
fuck a rain shower—it was hailing up in here. I strutted back
to the locker room to get ready to call it a night. Of course, I
got a bunch of eye rolls and dirty looks from the other
bitches, but maybe if they put some effort into their job,
they'd make more than a hundred dollars per night. I sepa-
rated what I owed to Montez, and once I was dressed in
regular clothes, I headed back to his office to hand off his cut.

Wanting nothing more than to hand this man his money
and go on about my business, I knew anything but that was
going to happen. I knew that there was no way he wasn't
gonna pick back up the conversation he had started before
my set.

"So, you don't got nothing to tell me?" Montez questioned
like I knew he would.

"No. What would I possibly have to talk to you about,
Montez?"

"Your favorite customer's girl calling up here, asking me to
give you a break. Does she know you be swallowing his dick
whole on the weekends? Let me find out y'all on that shit that
bitch Seven was singing about that had you bitches going
wild. On The Weekend or whatever it was. Tell me
something."

"Something," I replied flatly.

"Excuse me?" Montez said, confused.

"You're excused. Now can I go, or is there something else you would like to know?" Now that I knew that Fayth's overly sweet ass called up here on my behalf, it made me feel all the more bad for what used to take place in the private rooms here at Diamonds. She was truly a good girl, and I liked her. Never in a million years would I think I could get along with someone so pure and genuine, but maybe that was because I never took the time to meet anyone like Fayth.

"You're starting to feel real muthafuckin' confident these days, Trinity, like I won't replace you. Now what about Stefon? Any updates on what he's been planning?"

"The only thing he's talking about is moving the hell out of my house and into his own spot. Now if you don't mind, I have a stop I need to make for a friend before going home to my son." Without giving Montez room to say anything more, I walked out of his office and headed out to my car.

I had promised Fayth that I would stop by the hotel room she was staying in and bring her something to eat when I left the club, seeing she wasn't mobile. It was the least I could do after all she'd been through, some of which she didn't even know I played a part in. I placed an order online at Denny's so it would be ready for me to pick up. I hated being out in this city late at night. I mean, there were weirdos roaming the streets all hours of the day, but once it got dark, add some creeps with the weirdos.

Arriving to Fayth's room, I texted her to let her know I

was on my way up in the elevator so she would know it wasn't nobody but me knocking on her door. The way she was acting, you would think Jervon beat her ass and she wasn't in a car accident. All petrified and shit.

"I hope you eat meat," I told her, stepping into the room.

She laughed. "What makes you think I don't? And even if I didn't, I would tonight. I'm starving, and whatever you ordered smells delish."

Not wanting her to get up, I placed the bag on the small desk across from the two beds and pulled out her plate. I walked it over to her and noticed she was still wearing the hospital gown. "You should've asked me to bring you something to put on. I'm sure Stefon wouldn't even notice if I stole some of his sweats or gym shorts seeing as you have that cast."

"I didn't even think about it. I wish Jervon would just leave my damn house and go stay with that bitch. This shit is insane that he's been living a lie, and yet here I am stuck at hotel when his other woman has a house he can stay at. Do you think you could run to my house and grab me some of my things? I'll give you my key and pay you some money," Fayth asked me.

What I wanted to say was anything but what I allowed to come out my mouth. What she needed to hear was hiding from her problems and spending money wasn't going to make her situation disappear. She needed to just go home and face Jervon, but instead, I had given her my word that I would, in the morning, after dropping Lenny off with Mrs. Williams. It was bad enough that me and Stefon weren't really seeing eye to eye, but pissing him off by not coming right home tonight wasn't going to make things in our relationship any better.

When I made it home thirty-five minutes after saying bye to Fayth, I found Stefon wide awake, sitting on the sofa. The television wasn't on. It was dead silent. "What took you so long coming home?" he asked.

"I took Fayth something to eat. She's in that cast and can't move around well," I answered, walking toward the room so I could undress and hop in a shower.

"Don't go getting yourself caught up in other folks' mess, Trinity. That's my business partner, and if you piss him off, I'm screwed of a supplier," Stefon warned.

I didn't bother to answer him as I grabbed my robe and headed for the shower. By the time I finished in the bathroom and made it back to my room, he was already in the bed. Without saying a word, we both knocked out respectively on our own sides of the bed. You would've thought Trump came and put up a wall between us that was illegal if we crossed it instead of trying to build one to keep Mexicans out.

*The Next Morning*

"Bye, Dada," Lenny said as we were getting ready to walk out the door. I had the day off from the motel, but I wasn't going to tell Stefon that, because if he knew I was heading to Fayth and Jervon's house, he would have a fit after the remake I made the other night.

"Be good for Mrs. Williams, and Dada will have a prize for you later," Stefon told our son.

About a half an hour later, I was walking inside of the apartment that Fayth had given me the address to, and instantly regretted doing this favor for her. Her house smelled horrible. The trash was overflowing from the barrel. Half empty food containers were laying around everywhere with what looked like a fruit fly convention taking place. The sink was filled with dirty dishes. It was just disgusting. It almost looked like an abandoned house the homeless were sleeping in to keep warm at night. If it wasn't for the nice furnishings and the countless photos of Fayth and Jervon, I would question if I was at the right place. There was no way they were living like this.

Out of nowhere, Jervon appeared from the back, looking like trash himself. He could've been kin to Oscar the Grouch from *Sesame Street*. His facial hair was scruffy, his clothes were hanging off of him, and I could tell he was expecting to see Fayth standing in the doorway. His face dropped when he realized it wasn't anyone but me. He didn't even look embarrassed that I was standing in this filth he called home.

Jervon began grilling me about where his girl was and damn near begging me to help him convince her into returning home. He looked downright pathetic, so much so, I secretly snapped a few photos of the house and him to send to Fayth with hopes that she would feel bad and ask me to come get her and drive her back to her man. When I got a text back of her apologizing, saying she can't believe Jervon had the house in shambles because they both typically suffer from OCD, I decided to lend a helping hand. I mean, cleaning up people's mess was what I normally did during the day anyway.

"I don't even want to get involved in what you and Fayth have going on, Jervon. I only came here to grab her some clothes, seeing as she can't do it herself. But while I'm here, I'm gonna help you out as well by cleaning up in here. These toxic fumes can't be good for you to breathe in. Could you point me in the right direction of where Fayth keeps y'all cleaning products?"

"Trinity, can you please tell me where my wife is at?" Jervon begged, looking desperate.

"I can't tell you that. But I will talk to her and see if she will agree to meet up with you somewhere public to have a face to face conversation. But from the way she's been talking, I think it might be best if you just give her space and room to think. That's just my opinion as a woman. When Stefon caught me in bed with another man, that's what I did. He ran off somewhere, and I let him until he figured out if what I had done was worth throwing away our relationship. Now he's back, and we're slowly trying to rebuild. If the love you and Fayth share is the real deal, then she'll come around, but don't force her," I advised.

What I said seemed like it had given him some hope. He went to a door and opened it, revealing a small closet that seemed to be well stocked with almost every cleaning product you could think about. Seeing an opened set of yellow cleaning gloves, I put them on and got to work. It took me all of ninety minutes to dust, sweep floors, mop them, and put all the dishes away. All that was left was the three bags of trash to go wherever they threw their garbage. That was something I was going to have Jervon do.

Walking in the direction of where the bedroom he shared with Fayth was, I knocked and walked inside. He was on the phone with someone and had no shirt on. When I got closer and before I could ask him to take the trash out, I noticed he was on FaceTime with Stefon. As soon as Stefon got a glimpse of me, he blew up, automatically assuming the worst. Before hanging up without giving neither of us room to explain, he said, "I'm gonna fucking kill both of you for playing with my intelligence."

"Fuck!" Jervon said. "I done got us in some bullshit."

"I'll have Fayth explain to Stefon why I was over here. But I finished cleaning up. I'm gonna pack a bag to drop off to her. Can you at least take the garbage out?" I asked.

"Sure. Thank you, Trinity. I know this is weird for us to you know, umm, be around each other after what ummm, had happened between us in the past." Jervon stuttered.

"You're welcome, and please don't ever let either Stefon or Fayth know what used to go on at Diamonds. I don't want anyone to get hurt."

Jervon had agreed, while I looked through Fayth's clothes and decided on taking her more of those cheap nightgowns I guessed she liked, from Walmart, some shorts, and one pair of sweats that I thought belonged to Jervon. By the time I finished packing, Jervon made it back inside their apartment. We said our goodbyes, and I assured him that once I made it home, I would clarify things with Stefon. At least I hoped I was able to.

## Chapter Five

# JERVON

I tried to call Stefon back to explain what Trinity was doing at my house, even though she had assured me that she would handle it, but he didn't answer. I tried a few times but kept getting the same result. No matter what was going on, business had to continue, and we had to get to this money. I wasn't going to think too much of it because I had more pressing matters to focus on, like getting Fayth to come home. Her sending Trinity over here to pack up some of her shit made it clear to me that she didn't have no plans of returning home no time soon. I thought about what Trinity had suggested about me just leaving for a little bit and giving Fayth time to cool down, but by doing that, I felt like I was telling her I didn't care about her. That was anything but the truth. I loved her more than anything, even if I had a funny way of showing it.

Hearing my phone go off, I saw it was Shawnda hitting me up yet again. I knew I couldn't ignore her forever, for more than one reason, so I decided to hop in a shower, brush my teeth, and get myself together and head over to her house. But my first stop had to be the barber shop to get my shit lined up and looking fresh. Seeing Trinity look at me with disgust and then mentioning how I looked like a bum on the street, had me feeling stupid.

I probably gained a good ten pounds from all the takeout food I'd been consuming the last few days, but that didn't stop me from stopping at KFC and grabbing something to eat when I left from getting my lineup. Instead of going through the drive thru, I decided to get out my car and go inside to eat and give myself time to think before I get to Shawnda's house. I knew this conversation I was about to have with her was gonna be a long, sensitive situation. The last thing I wanted was to go back and forth with her crazy ass.

Deciding on a three-piece meal with two sides of mashed potatoes, I found a seat in a corner and got as comfortable as possible. Trying my luck, I tried to get ahold of Fayth, but like every other attempt, I failed. Not talking to her was really messing with my mental. I missed her scent. I was craving her touch. I needed to hear her voice outside of the bland recording she had on her voicemail. And I couldn't even hear that now, because her mailbox was full, from all my previous messages.

When I got to Shawnda's house, I sat in my car for a few minutes, contemplating if I should just turn back around and go home or not. Getting involved with this woman had been nothing but a mistake from day one, but now that she revealed she was carrying my baby, it made everything complicated. Her getting pregnant was never part of the plan, and I'd been trying to figure out how it even happened. Every time we were intimate, I used protection, and not once did I recall the condom breaking. Ironically, Shawnda had just told me about the baby the same night Fayth found me over here, and the part about me and Shawnda getting married before she gave birth was news to me. We damn sure never discussed that.

Knowing I had to get this conversation over with, I got out and went inside. I found Shawnda sitting down in her den, and I took a seat. There was a long awkward silence for about five minutes, neither one of us saying shit to the other, just facing one another, I guess trying to read the other's mind. I didn't know if she was able to pick up on anything I was thinking, but I damn sure was coming up empty. Deciding to finally speak up, I said, "Shawnda, we need to talk."

The second I spotted her leg bouncing, I knew we were about to have anything but an adult conversation. "You damn right we do. Are you ready to explain to me where you've been the last seven days and where do we stand? I hope you broke things off with that woman too."

"Listen, first of all, I need for you to calm down and keep an open mind about things. The reason I didn't leave Fayth when I met you is because she had a mental breakdown and threatened to commit suicide. I've been trying to get her therapy for a few months now. I need you to understand I can't just leave her. I'm responsible for her."

"How are you responsible for a grown ass woman, Jervon? You need to come a little stronger than that, baby."

"Easy. I'm not trying to have her death on my conscience for the rest of my life. I'll rather push her to leave me than me leave her and she does something crazy. She still hasn't returned home, and I have no idea of her whereabouts, so she could've moved back home to Alabama to live with her ghetto ass mama. If that's the case, then we will be good and be a happy family. But in the event Fayth does come around and is just healing in a hospital somewhere, then I need for you to be patient."

I was lying my ass off and was doing my best to lay it on thick. Shawnda smirked and said, "Blah. Blah. Blah. Excuses is all I keep hearing from you, Jervon. What do you think I am? One of these stupid bitches that's running around these streets? You know me better than that. I'm way smarter than that, so you must've known coming over here running that ridiculous story wasn't gonna fly. I don't know if I'm madder at the fact you are engaged to that bitch or that you really trying to sit in my face and lie."

"Shawnda, you don't think I want to be here and work on our growing family? Come on and give me the benefit of the doubt. Whose bed was I sleeping in damn near every night? Not Fayth's. I was here with you. The only reason I haven't been back since that night is because I have been trying to locate Fayth. But I'm here now and explaining everything to you," I pleaded. To me, I sounded very convincing, and if I were in her shoes, then I'd be beaming with joy. Not everything I said was entirely false. I mean, I was in Shawnda's bed most nights, but I was also with Fayth as well. I just had each one of them thinking I was at work when I wasn't at home with them.

Standing up, she shouted, "You know what? Just get the fuck out of my house! I ain't trying to hear all this bullshit. It's too much for me, and I honestly don't see myself sitting around while you play this cat and mouse game with another bitch. I'm too grown and have too much to lose fucking around with you! You're the biggest mistake I have made in my life, and I can't stand you. Now please get the hell out my house, and furthermore, out of my life!"

This wasn't going in the direction I needed it to go at all. Having Shawnda canceling me from her life meant she'd no longer supply me with the pills I had Stefon pushing. Granted, I really didn't need to be selling drugs, because my secret was out the bag with Fayth. She now knew I lost my job at the hospital, but just like I got hooked on watching strippers shake their ass, I was addicted to the fast, easy money of supplying the streets with narcotics.

I got up and grabbed ahold of Shawnda's hands and gave her the evilest look I could muster up without actually being upset. "I'm not going any damn where, especially now that you're having my baby."

She pushed me away when I tried to kiss her on her neck, which was her sensitive spot, and said, "I can't stand you!"

I grabbed her again and started to kiss on her. But the more my lips landed on hers, the more she tried to resist by crying out that she hated me. Eventually, Shawnda started to kiss me back. One thing led to another thing, and I had her laid out on the sofa while I started to eat her pussy then moved on to her ass, something I had never even tried on Fayth, but Shawnda loved it.

When I climbed in her tight pussy, it felt like heaven. It had been so long since I had sex I was feeling backed up. I really needed some pussy. Shawnda's cries continued while I was stroking her. "I can't stand you, Jervon. I hate you."

I went deeper and harder while kissing on her neck before looking her straight in her eyes. "Do you mean that? Do you really hate me?"

She started to nod her head and replied, "Yeah."

Asking her yet again, I said, "So you hate me, huh?"

"Yeah."

Her mouth was confirming that she couldn't stand me, but her eyes were telling a completely different story. "Tell me you hate me one more time," I told her while I picked up the pace and was now hammering in and out of her love tunnel.

"I love you!" Shawnda moaned out like I knew she would. Smiling, I tossed her legs over my shoulders while grabbing ahold of hers as I began pounding her; that way, she got the whole dick in her stomach, while my balls were slapping against her ass. That shit was feeling so good I could no longer hold back anymore.

"You better cum with me because I can't hold off much

longer." I warned her, and a few pumps later, I was letting off inside her while she screamed out she was cumming. I released her legs and started to kiss her, realizing I had just fucked her without a condom for the first time. But I had nothing to worry about because she was already pregnant, according to the paper she showed me last week.

I couldn't lie; fucking Shawnda raw made me realize that being with her wouldn't be so bad after all. If Fayth didn't forgive me and refused to work things out, then at least I still had Shawnda. She was almost as pretty as Fayth. But when it came down to bodies, Shawnda's was real and thick as hell. Her pussy was fire too.

But regardless how good life could be with someone like Shawnda, the heart wanted what it wanted, and that was Fayth. She held all the power over my love, and I had none to give to any other woman, no matter how good they were.

"We're gonna be alright," I assured Shawnda but then realized she had fallen asleep. I got up to go into the kitchen to get some water before heading to the bathroom upstairs to brush my teeth. I washed up with a rag and then went to get Shawnda up so she could come to the bed. But before joining her in the bedroom, I tried Fayth one more time but got her voicemail. Nothing new.

*Chapter Six*

# FAYTH

As soon as Trinity let me know that Jervon caved and agreed to leave our shared apartment, I returned home and immediately had the building management have the locks changed. Now I'd been hiding out in this house for way too long, and I was started to go crazy. Not only was I bored, but I was lonely. I really needed for this leg to hurry up and heal so I could get out and start looking for a new car. It was still shocking how I lost so much in a matter of a few hours. My fiancée, my car, my respect, my future. I damn near had to start over from scratch and really didn't know what I wanted to do with my life next.

I knew that being around people would do me right because the way I had been isolating myself wasn't helping matters. It was as if I was locked away in some prison but in solitary confinement because I'd been alone for far too long.

Even inmates had some sort of communication with humans, whereas I'd been avoiding them. Even Trinity. Just comparing my circumstances to some prisoners made me start to feel bad. Here I was, free with the ability to walk, well hop, out of my door and take on the world, and they had that right taken away from them.

To me, my reasons made sense on why I was avoiding the public. For one, the big ass scar on my face from the steering wheel. Two, I had this large bulky cast weighing me down. Three, although Boston was a pretty big city, it was still small when you didn't want it to be, and the thought of bumping into Jervon made me sick. Knowing I couldn't sulk about my pitiful circumstances no longer, I decided to hit up Trinity and see if she wanted to come over and hang out with me.

"Girl, you are alive. I was about to send someone over to make sure you weren't dead," Trinity said, picking up my call.

I laughed at how dramatic she sounded. "I know, and I'm sorry for my horrible communication skills, but that's why I'm calling you now, to see if you wanted to come over and have some wine with me."

While I waited for her to respond, I silently prayed she agreed because, now that I had her on the phone, I realized just how much I needed to unwind with a glass of my favorite red wine. "Yeah, but I have to bring Lenny with me, if you don't mind. Stefon is out handling something with Jervon."

Hearing that man's name made the hair on the back of my neck stand at attention. "That's no problem. I'll order some pizza or something," I told her.

"Sounds great. See you in about thirty minutes or so," Trinity replied before disconnecting the call. And just like she said, half hour later, she was knocking on my door with Pizza Hut right behind her with our food.

Looking down at her son, I couldn't help but to smile. He was such a handsome little boy who looked exactly like Trinity. "I would've been here like ten minutes ago, but Lenny made me pack a bag of toys to bring. This child hates going places and have to sit still in front of the TV."

"Well that's a good thing that he likes to be active because one of the leading causes of child obesity these days is due to the parents allowing television and electronics to keep their kids busy. Excuse me while I get me a slice of pizza before I start drinking this wine. The last thing I want to be doing tonight is hugging the toilet with a messed-up leg getting in my way," I joked.

An hour after we started to drink, I was cracking open another bottle of the pricey wine that Jervon had purchased a few years ago. He always admired those rich folks that bought houses that had a wine cellar and wanted to start his collection before we even bought our own. Well now, here I was enjoying the strong yet delicious bottles he had.

Lenny was showing signs that he was getting tired, so I offered up my bed for Trinity to lay him in while we got comfortable on my living room floor. The music was on low, and the vibe was serene. I was really feeling relaxed and happy for the first time in almost two weeks. Or maybe it was the alcohol in my system that gave me this warm feeling, but before I was able to stop myself, I blurted out, "The night of the accident, I had sex with another man."

The shocked expression on Trinity's face made me start laughing hard and loud. I guess in a way, it was funny, because here I was refusing to talk to Jervon because of his infidelity when I did the same. "Wait? What exactly do you have me in here drinking? I think I'm hallucinating and hearing things. I swear I just heard you say you cheated on Jervon. When and with who?" Trinity questioned.

"Before I had ran into you at your job, and with who doesn't really matter because look at what Jervon was doing to me all along. And girl, it was some of the best sex I have ever had in my life. There's been a few nights I've laid in bed and played with myself, replaying the positions he had me in." Just saying those words brought a flood of images into my mind of sexy ass Montez and the way he was drilling into me like he hated me.

We kicked it for a little while longer before Lenny started to get restless. Trinity called up Stefon and asked him to come pick them up because she had been drinking and didn't want to drive with their son while under the influence. I couldn't make out what he was saying on the other end, but the way Trinity started to smile, I knew it was nasty. Seeing it made me miss having someone I could turn to when the mood struck, but it was what it was. Not long after, Stefon was knocking on the door, and before I unlocked it, I made him promise he was alone. It wouldn't surprise me if Jervon tried to tag along with hopes of me letting him come in to talk.

Stefon went and picked up Lenny, who decided to pass out after all while Trinity bagged up all the Hot Wheel cars he had brought with him. Before walking out the door, Trinity made me promise that I wouldn't stay a stranger and to call her again soon. I had to admit, I really did have fun, and having a female friend was turning out to be something great. I never really experienced the whole best friend thing. Even in college. Many of the girls disliked me simply because the handsome, bright, and soon to be doctor Jervon loved me. Or so I thought he did.

The next morning, the ringing of my phone woke me up, and I instantly grabbed my head from the massive headache I had from what I was certain was the first sign of a hangover from hell. "Hello," I answered groggily.

"Hey, boo. I was just calling to see how you were feeling. Me and Stefon couldn't help but to laugh the whole way home last night from how fucked up you were. His ass actually blamed me, like I was the one who kept pouring you glass after glass and not the other way around," Trinity said, laughing.

"Why did you let me consume so much? I feel stuck right now."

"You had a good time, and that's all that matters. But I'm calling because Stefon is gonna run me by there to grab my car, and I thought I'd call to see if you needed anything."

That was nice of her, but unless she could deliver a time machine for me to climb into, then I didn't need anything. "No. I'm about to get up and take something for this headache. I feel like someone is bouncing rocks off the top of my dome."

"Do you have Bayer?" she asked.

"No. I think all I have is Excedrin and Tylenol."

"Don't take either of those. I'll run up and bring you Bayer. Trust me. It's the best thing for a hangover." Who was I to debate, even if I was the one who went to school for medicine? Trinity was the one that worked in a club and clearly could handle her liquor.

Stumbling from the bed to the bathroom, I had just finished brushing my teeth, rinsing my mouth with Listerine, and washing my face, when Trinity knocked at the door. She came in full of energy, carrying a tray with both a tea and coffee for me, and handed me the bag from CVS with a bottle of Bayer. Deciding on the tea over the coffee, I opened the bottle and popped two pills.

"I was thinking about something, and please don't judge me or laugh, but would you be willing to teach me how to dance? Now that I got this body, I may as well put some use to it and start stripping alongside you. That is, if you don't mind." I wasn't even sure where that came from because, up until the words spilled from my mouth, the thought never crossed my mind.

Still standing at the door, Trinity appeared to be in deep thought before replying. "How about this? You can come to work with me tomorrow night and see for yourself what goes on behind the scenes, and if you still want to give it a shot, I'll gladly show you some moves. But I promise you, there's so much more than meets the eye when it comes to the stripping world."

"Sounds like a plan. Thank you for everything. I don't know how I would be getting by if it weren't for you."

Trinity smiled then left out the door, leaving me alone. Knowing I had just made plans for the following night, I needed to get myself right, starting with my hair, nails, lashes and brows. Looked like I'd be spending some money on Ubers to get me around all day. Lucky for me, we had a stand-up shower in the adjoined bathroom where I could shower.

While I waited for my first ride to show up, I checked the balance in the joint account me and Jervon once shared, and to my surprise, he made not one but two decent sized deposits in the last two weeks. Seeing that amount, I knew just what card I would be swiping during my excursion today. If you asked me, I deserved to take all of Jervon's damn money and spend it after I wasted years of my life on his ass. Not only was I treating myself on the previously mentioned services to feel better for myself, but I was gonna make a stop down Copley to get something to wear tomorrow night.

Five hours later and ready to rip my freshly installed hair out of my head from my pain level being through the roof, I grabbed my phone and decided to spend the rest of the night on social media. I had a few photos that Jervon had snapped of me post op but clearly before my car accident. I uploaded those and then added a new profile picture of me that I had taken today after leaving the salon. I changed my status from engaged to single and set all other photos to where only I could see them. What I didn't do was block Jervon because I wanted him to suffer, watching every move I made from this day forward. The sweet naïve Fayth died in that wreck, and a bad bitch was born.

Trinity had agreed to come over and help me cut the hideous looking cast from my leg before we headed out to Diamonds. I had assumed that Trinity would have me shadowing her around the club as she made rounds, but I soon found out she wanted me to witness the catty behavior of all the other girls backstage. Sitting in the locker room, it was like a revolving door, and every time one dancer came in excited about how much money they were able to sucker from a customer, another was exiting, talking about they were gonna top it.

"When did Montez hire a house mother, and how long have you been dancing?" one girl asked me while checking me out from head to toe.

"Excuse me?" I replied, not really understanding what she meant by her first question.

"When... did... Montez... hire... a... house... mother? There. Did you understand now that I slowed it down for you?" Before I could respond, she turned to another girl that was just finishing her makeup and added, "It's always the cute ones that's dumb as fuck."

I had to laugh to keep myself from going off because, if I was going to see about getting a job eventually at Diamonds, I didn't want to start off with enemies. "I'm not sure what a house mother is exactly, and to answer the other question, I've never stripped a day in my life. I'm a friend of Trinity's."

"Ooh, that bitch finna be in trouble as soon as I find Montez and let him know that she got her people hanging out in the back. I'm so tired of Trinity thinking because she busts that pussy open for the boss that she can do what she wants," the same girl said, storming out to find Montez, if I had to take a guess.

Sure enough, not even five minutes later, in walked his fine ass, and when he noticed it was me sitting there, he smiled. "What brings you here, Fayth?" he asked, and the smirk on the hater's face dropped with the quickness once she realized that Montez knew who I was and didn't yell for me to get out.

"I asked Trinity to show me all that goes down in her world because I was thinking about, once my leg heals some more, coming to dance."

Rubbing his hands together, he nodded his head and said, "Is that right? How about you give me a private dance? A pre-audition. You know, that way I can see how much you learn from Trinity by comparing your performance tonight and then later when you come back."

I allowed Montez to help me to my feet, and as we were walking out from the back, I spotted Jervon enjoying a dance from some girl. They were smiling a little too much, and instantly it got my blood boiling. "You know what I'd much rather do than dance for you? I'd rather fuck."

"You ain't said nothing but a word, but I have a quick run

to make, so come take that ride with me, and we can stop some place and make it do what it do."

Slowly limping alongside Montez, I let him lead the way out the door while never taking my eyes off of the man I was once engaged to. My heart was racing, and it felt like he was stabbing it all over again. I hated that I still loved him deeply, but we were about to be on the same level. It was time for me to play his game and enjoy doing it.

I knew Montez said he had someplace he had to go first, but that didn't go as planned, because the second we were seated in his car, I reached over and freed his precious cargo. If I was going to be honest with myself, I had never seen a dick so pretty in all my adult years. Not that I had seen many in person, but porn was once my best friend and lover.

"Damn, girl, you ain't playing," he said, guiding my head down to his meat. I loved a man who stayed smelling fresh. If I didn't know any better, I'd say that Montez had just stepped out of the shower because his dick smelled like men's body-wash. That only made my mouth wetter, which in turn helped me suck him off better.

While I was bobbing and weaving, I forced his hand to release my hair and brought it down to my pussy that was purring for his touch. Montez barely grazed my hooded lady when I felt myself already cumming. It was crazy how a simple touch from someone you knew nothing much about could make you feel things someone you spent years with had to work to achieve.

"Man, fuck this. Watch out. I'm about to tear that little

pussy up," Montez said while stopping me just before he came. He got out the car and made his way around it. While he was doing that, I got out and went to the back seat so I could lay down while being careful not to bang my broken leg and cause damage.

Right there in the open parking lot, with one door open and Montez on top of me, fucking me like we were alone somewhere, I was hollering and screaming as tidal wave after tidal wave escaped from my body so easily. I was seeing stars, and not because I had x-ray vision and could see through the roof of the car, but because of how lightheaded I was feeling from the multiple orgasms Montez was causing in such a few moments time.

"Damn, bitch, this pussy is good. Even better than I remembered." Montez grunted as he filled the condom I didn't even see him put on. He must've done that when he was walking around his car. He slid off me and helped me get from the back seat and into the front. I'd never done anything so wild and spontaneous like this, and I liked it. I think what made it all the more better was the risk of being caught by someone. Specifically, Jervon.

I asked Montez to drop me off at my house while I sent Trinity a message, telling her my leg was hurting, and I left my pain medication at home. I knew she wouldn't get the message until she returned from the floor, because her phone was put up in her locker.

## Chapter Seven
# MONTEZ

I was down Copley, going in and out of stores, trying to find the perfect gift for my granny. Tonight, the family was hosting her seventy-fifth birthday party, and there was no way I was showing up empty handed with just cash money. My granny didn't play that bullshit. She wouldn't accept it. I learned the hard way a few years back when I first started to make a name for myself. Just like today, I waited until the last minute on picking out something and figured I'd hand her some money to go shopping. The look she gave me let me know I had done fucked up. In her opinion, it lacked thought and effort. Her words were something along the lines of, "I would have loved a card with no money over this thousand dollars because it would mean you took your time to find the perfect one."

Seeing all these insanely priced shoes and purses that were designed for younger women made me think that maybe opening up a high-end shop that catered to elderly ladies that were still young at heart and fashionable, like my granny, won't be a bad idea. Some shoes that wouldn't cause them to break a hip but would still have smooth ass Slick Rick from the barber shop willing to sign over his disability and see a doctor about some Viagra to impress them.

Who better to contact about what to get than the queen herself, so I called her just to pick her brain. "Hey, sugar, what you calling me for? You know I'm over at Pearly-Mae's getting my hair done for tonight, so I hope this is important."

"You're gonna have all eyes on you no matter how you look, but I wanted to see how old you are by testing your skills. What do you think your favorite grandson got you for your birthday? If you get it right, then I will be your date Thursday night for bingo."

"You ain't slick, boy. I hear the music in the background. You're standing in the middle of some store unsure of what you're gonna get for me. Follow your heart, and I'll see you tonight, baby. Oh, and clear that schedule for Thursday because I know I guessed right." And with that, she hung up. How the hell did she know me so well?

Well, that idea got me absolutely nowhere. I was no closer to finding something than I was five minutes ago, and now I had to endure a bunch of old ass women staring at me as I played bingo. The corny shit I got myself caught up in, but only for my granny because not even my mama was gonna have me doing some lame boring shit like that.

"Fancy seeing you here," I heard from behind, and when I spun around, I saw it was Fayth.

"What a sight for sore eyes. Aye, I need some help picking out a gift. Do you got time to help a brother out?" I asked.

Right away, her smiled dropped, and like a typical female, she automatically assumed some shit. "How you gonna ask me to help you find something for one of your bitches?"

"Hold that thought while I call my granny and let her know that you called her a bitch," I joked. And just like I knew, her facial expression changed again, but this time, guilt consumed it.

"I'm sorry. I just thought... never mind, it's not important. Tell me a little about her and a price range, and I'll be happy to assist you, Montez. But you have to do something for me first."

I was curious as to what favor she wanted to trade for mine, but if it was giving her some of this golden stick I possessed, then I'd have no problem. It would just have to wait because, right now, I didn't have the time to be playing in her guts. Fayth's pussy was too good to have just a quickie. "And what's that?"

"Carry these bags, because my arms are starting to hurt."

Looking down, I had to ask her what she did for work to be able to shop at so many high-end stores. Let me find out she was connected to a cartel or something along those lines. "I see you balling. Let me get a loan."

Fayth laughed, but I was serious. I was no expert when it came to buying women's shit, but I knew enough to know that most of these labels she had bags to cost a few thou-sand dollars. And as I mentioned, she had about six bags. "The more money my ex deposits into our joint account, the more I'm going to spend it to cover for my pain and suffer-ing," Fayth stated while shrugging her shoulders. I made a mental note not to ever get in to deep with her ass and piss her off.

Within thirty minutes, Fayth was instructing a salesperson at the Chanel counter inside of Neimen Marcus to ring up what she described as a flap bag with handles. I had no clue how much it cost, but from the way the women who worked there eyed Fayth, questioning her, I knew it was gonna run me more than I had anticipated on spending.

"It's for his grandmother," Fayth stated, and I didn't understand her need.

The lady smiled and voiced, "It's a very nice handbag. I wish my grandson could afford to give me something as nice. Luckily for you, it's on sale today to make room for newer merchandise."

When I saw the price on the register say $3,300, I thought it was the before price and she hadn't knocked off the differ-ence, but that wasn't the case. The shit went for over four racks. I wasn't going to make a big deal out of it in front of the stranger, and truthfully, my granny was worth that and so much more, but what the hell was the big deal with these damn purses for them to cost so much.

As we were getting ready to leave, I asked Fayth where she had parked at so I could carry her bags for her. "I don't have a car. I still haven't found one that I like enough or that I can really afford."

That shit didn't make no damn sense, seeing as she was up in these stores spending money on bullshit. I wanted to voice that to her, but it really wasn't my money she was wasting stupidly. "You can't be taking the subway with all these bags as unbalanced as you are right now. Some muthafucka gonna see you limping and rob yo' ass. Let me drop you off at home. What you should be doing is bringing all this shit back and putting money down on a car." I couldn't help myself and had to drop that last part out there.

On the drive to her house, we chopped it up, and I hated to admit it, but I really liked her energy. She was a cool ass female but was dealt a fucked-up hand when she got with her ex. That muthafucka really fucked with her mental and had her thinking she wasn't good enough to commit to. Granted, before she gotten her body done, she was cute in the face, but that was all, and working at a gas station didn't really impress me. But knowing all of what I did know, I had to admit that muthafucka was a fool. Fayth had the brains to go with the body.

Before letting Fayth exit out of my car, a last-minute gift idea crossed my mind. My granny always got on my ass for showing up to family events without anyone on my arm, and I knew bringing someone as beautiful as Fayth, who could hold a bright intelligent conversation, would please her. Sadly, the men in our family always thought with our dicks and not our brains, so the women they all brought home to meet Granny wasn't worth shit. Look at Trinity. The bitch took her damn clothes off in my club and cleaned up dirty hotel rooms during the day.

"What you got going on tonight?" I asked Fayth.

"Nothing but watching *Greys Anatomy* like I've been doing."

"Well, change of plans. You wanna be my plus one, that way you can see my granny's face when she opens up her gift?" I still couldn't believe I was asking this shit, but it was what it was. I liked shorty.

"Are you sure?" Fayth asked.

"Baby, I ain't the type of man to play games. You should know that much about me. I say what is on my mind, and I really don't want to be the talk of the room for showing up alone another year in a row. This time, I want the elders to have something decent to say, and with a nice female who knows how to present herself on my arm, I know it'll give them tons to gossip about."

Fayth agreed and added, "I actually just bought a really cute outfit today and had no idea where I was going to wear it to. I guess we were destined to run into one another."

I didn't want her getting the wrong idea and thinking we were about to be like one of those urban book couples I hear the bitches in the dressing room at work talking about. The last thing on my mind was making anyone my wife. Fayth was just cool people with good pussy. "Be ready at six."

When we walked into the function hall on Mount Vernon in Dorchester, all eyes were on Fayth. It was like I didn't even exist. Especially Stefon and Trinity. It was like they'd seen a ghost. To make matters worse, when Lenny looked to see why everyone had gotten quiet and seen me, he jumped off his father's lap and came flying across the room into my arms. Naturally, that caused tension in the room as Trinity came over and snatched him from me. This funny ass hoe used to love when I would play with Lenny when Stefon abandoned them. Now she was gonna act like me giving him attention was a bad thing.

"You fucking up by getting involved with Montez. I hope this isn't who you were talking about the other night," Trinity whispered in Fayth's ear but not low enough to where I couldn't hear what she said.

Just when I was about to say something, my granny walked up to us and whisked me and Fayth across the room. She already knew there was bad blood between me and Stefon and that Trinity was the cause of it, so she must've known that me being here with another female would only complicate matters more. But she had no idea how much so. The fact that Trinity and Fayth knew one another enough to where Fayth called to the club didn't move me one bit. I didn't think seeing her with me would bother Trinity either, but I guess I thought wrong.

Now that we were seated alone, well, away from my cousin and his bitch I should say, Fayth asked, "What was that all about? Why aren't we sitting near Trinity and your cousin?"

I had to take a second to fill her in on how her little friend really got down. Fayth's eyes grew in size when I told her how me and Trinity were fucking for a year and only stopped recently when Stefon came back. "Question is, why are you friends with Trinity?" I asked her.

"Why shouldn't I be?" Fayth answered my question with a question of her own.

I was about to let her know that Trinity was the number one bitch in the club that was sucking Jervon's dick, when my granny came back over to formally meet Fayth. "And who is this young lady, Montez?"

"Granny, this is my friend, Fayth. Fayth, this is the only woman besides my mama and auntie Ruth in my life." I introduced the two.

"Nice to meet you, ma'am. I thought for a minute you might've been Montez's mother. There is no way you're the guest of honor and celebrating your seventy-fifth birthday." Fayth smiled as she spoke to my granny.

"Oh, I like her Montez, but yes, baby. You know the saying —black don't crack. Granny still got it, don't she, baby?" my granny said.

My phone started to ring, and I saw it was Laron calling me from his private phone. "Excuse me while I take this call," I said to the two of them, walking away. I looked back just to make sure that Fayth was OK, and the two of them were both looking at me and laughing at something Granny had said. I could only imagine, but I'd be sure to ask Fayth when I returned.

When I reached the hallway that led to the bathrooms, I answered. "Talk to me."

"So, check it out. A'Kirah just called me crying," Laron said.

"I don't give a fuck what she was doing, Laron. Ain't shit changed. When I find that bitch, she better have a good explanation on why she was in my damn club, or it's lights out for her!" I yelled but not loud enough for any of the guests to hear me.

"Man, just listen to me. Damn. She sounded clean and was saying something about someone blackmailing her into helping him take everything you own. She wants to fix things and is willing to tell you all you need to know but wants to make sure you can protect her if she does."

"Listen, if she calls you back, tell her I need names and locations on everyone involved. I don't care that she's your kid's mother. I'll kill whoever stands in the way. Just make sure she's not trying to set me up, and if the information she has is all that she claims it to be, then yes, I will see to it that whoever this muthafucka is that's out for me, won't hurt her. We can send her and your kid out of state."

My mouth was telling his ass that, but in my head, I knew I was gonna have to kill her anyway. I just wasn't gonna let him know.

## Chapter Eight
## STEFON

I couldn't believe who the fuck Montez had done brought to my granny's birthday party. I was talking about really in disbelief. The way Jervon used to brag about Fayth, I couldn't help but to wonder how the hell she landed on the arm of someone like my cousin. Montez and Jervon were complete opposites, and that only let me know one thing about Ms. Fayth: She didn't have a specific type. There was no way she could. But regardless of all that, one question still remained: How in the hell did those two meet?

When the perfect moment hit, I snapped a picture of Fayth and Montez, sitting extremely close, and sent it to Jervon. I knew if I had just told him that she appeared to be moving on, he wouldn't just take my word on it. For a few weeks now, he'd been lying to everyone, including himself, by saying that Fayth was just trying to prove a point to him, but she'd be allowing him back in the house once she cooled off. Seeing her with my womanizer cousin, I knew it was all over for Jervon. Once Montez got his claws into a female, it was hard for her to shake him. Look at what happened between him and Trinity. If we didn't have a son together, I knew that Trin wouldn't have looked my way again.

Thirty seconds after I hit send, Jervon hit me back, asking where we were at. I was on the fence about giving him the address because coming up in here making a scene with all this family around would prove to be the dumbest thing he would ever do in his life. Shit, Jervon couldn't fuck with Montez, even if it were the two of them alone. Jervon thought he was doing something that day he hemmed me up in the warehouse, but little did he know, I saw more fear in his eyes than he thought he placed in me. That man wasn't cut from the same cloth as me, no matter how much he thought he had the ability to hurt someone. The only lives he was responsible for were the ones he mistreated medically.

I texted Jervon the address with a strong warning to not come up in here on no foolishness because, at the end of the day, I had to side with Montez. At least in this room full of our kinfolk I had to. I wasn't going to war with all the cousins behind someone I just started to do business with.

Right after I put my phone down, I spotted Montez walk away and head toward the restrooms with his phone in hand. Ironically, Trinity also had just left, using the excuse she had to use the ladies' room. Shit seemed a little to coincidental for my liking, so I placed Lenny on his feet and pointed out my mother for him to go run over to, and I went to see what those two had going on. I didn't have to round the corner to know that it was only my paranoia kicking in when I heard Montez on the phone talking to Laron, so I walked back over to take my seat at my assigned table. What I really wanted to do was go have a word with Fayth because she appeared to be too sweet of a girl to get wrapped up in the likes of my no-good ass cousin.

Trinity finally returned back from her little bathroom break, and I couldn't help but to look at her suspiciously. "What took you so long?" I asked.

"Come outside with me real quick. I don't want to talk here where someone can hear us."

She sounded serious, so I approached my mother and asked her to stay with Lenny while me and Trinity went outside in the car to have a smoke. My mother was cool as shit and knew that smoking helped keep me calm, so naturally, she agreed. Once we were settled in the car, Trinity broke down how she was just about to leave from the restroom when she heard Montez talking on the phone, so she stayed back to hear what he was saying.

"At first, I was hoping I could catch him sweet talking another female so I could go over to Fayth and let her hear, but I quickly learned he wasn't speaking to a female. Stefon, please tell me the truth about A'Kirah. Are you sure she isn't working with you, because if she is, then all hell is about to break out! She is willing to turn on whoever was behind her going to the club that night, and you know once Montez and

Laron knows who is out to take them down, they gonna attack first."

I was unsure of all of what was going on and just as confused now as I was when Trinity brought her ass home from work early one night, grilling me about why A'Kirah was at Diamonds and what was my role in it. I told her then, and I was trying to tell her now that whatever, or whoever I should say, had A'Kirah working with them, had nothing to do with me. I'd never trust a dope fiend to do spy work, because they'd always switch up. They couldn't be trusted for shit.

At first, I was going to just dismiss all the information my girl just gave me, but I had too much riding for me to ignore it. It wasn't that I wanted to go do some digging to see what I could find out to help my cousin like the old days. I needed to get to the bottom of it to protect my own ass. Me and Montez may be cousins but were brought up like brothers, and I knew if someone was gunning for me the way it seemed like someone was for him, then I was making sure I came out on top.

Granted, I had my own agenda for getting back at his ass for betraying me, but it didn't involve him dying or even going to prison for life. Just take something that meant the world to him: his reputation. Montez was known to say his word was all he had, and if he didn't have that, then he didn't have shit. Well I wanted to paint him out to the city as the bitch he really was.

"Sit right here while I go get Lenny from my mother. I'm gonna lie and tell her and Granny that something you ate isn't agreeing with you so we leaving," I told Trinity as I exited the car and headed inside.

The whole ride to the house, I was plotting in my head on how I was going to take control of things before the situation got out of hand. Staying two steps ahead of everyone was key for my plan to work. Going against my cousin was one thing, but in order for everything to work out the way I was envisioning, I had to ensure that Rodney kept his cool as well. My plan in the end was for Rodney to be revealed as the snake and Montez take him out, but not before Rodney showed everyone Montez's true colors. That would leave me to be the victorious one.

"What are you up to, Stefon?" Trinity questioned, breaking me from my thoughts.

"Nothing for you to worry about. I just need to figure out what is going on before it fucks with all I'm trying to do for our future. That's all," I assured her.

As I carried my now sleeping son up the stairs and into the apartment, I could tell from Trinity's aura that she had something on her mind she wanted to say. "Say what's on your mind, Trin."

"I'm just worried, that's all. I really wish you would just put all that hatred you feel for Montez behind you and forgive him like you did me. Y'all share the same blood, and a war ain't worth it."

"Have more faith in your man, baby. The same way Montez won't hurt my mama by something happening to me, I ain't trying to hurt his. I'm the last person he got to worry about trying to take his life, but I have an idea on who it is, and I'm going to see what I can do to get them to back off." What I had just said wasn't a complete lie. I knew who was after my cousin, and truthfully, I was working with him, but it seemed like we weren't on the same page. Rodney getting A'Kirah to find out information wasn't part of the plan. "But listen, I have to go make a few moves and check on some things, and I'll be back. Keep the door locked, and don't answer it for nobody."

Without having to think too hard, I went right to Rodney's house to see what he had to do with A'Kirah. I couldn't think of anyone outside of him that wanted to fuck with Montez, so it only made sense. And if I was correct, then that meant his cover was about to blown once A'Kirah met up with Laron and Montez.

"What the fuck you doing here?" Rodney asked once he came to his door. We had agreed never to be spotted together so that word wouldn't get back to either crew, his or Montez's, that we had dealings, so seeing me on his porch pissed him off.

"Aye, if you got anything to do with that bitch A'Kirah, you better get it under control. Word is she's ready to talk and is supposed to be meeting up with her baby daddy to tell who she working with." I warned Rodney.

Before he could say anything back, my phone went off, and it was my mother calling, so I answered to make sure everything was okay. "Son, who is this man that's here looking for you? He is claiming he's your friend and you invited him."

Shit. I had forgot all about Jervon! "Ma, don't let him in without me there to do damage control. Just tell him I had an emergency, and I'll hit his line up shortly. And whatever you do, Ma, don't let Montez see him."

"That dumb bitch." Rodney mumbled as I put my phone back in my pocket, letting me know that he was indeed working with her.

"I can't believe you were stupid enough to ask someone like A'Kirah for help. What help could she possibly provide to what you're trying to accomplish? Even before she got on drugs, Laron kept her away from anything that had to do with Montez's business."

"I had her go up in Diamonds and hide a camera in the locker room. She was supposed to get him to let her into his office too and plant one in there as well, but she said she panicked and ran out. I told you I'm taking every damn thing from his ass. Every dollar, every penny." Rodney seethed.

And here I thought this man had some common sense. Or even had a clue about who the fuck Montez was when it came down to not only business but who he allowed close to him. Anybody who held a simple conversation with him knew he would never allow the drugged-out version of A'Kirah remotely close to his club, let alone office to plant cameras. "Well, I hope you're prepared because if not, suit up and get ready. Your little friend is about to tell everything to save herself."

Rodney ran his hand down his face, deep in thought before he looked at me and said, "Look, I need your help, and it can't wait. We have to move fast. I'm killing that bitch tonight."

I really didn't have a choice because, if not, then A'Kirah would be running her dick suckers to gain brownie points, and everything I'd been working so hard to achieve would be for nothing. I was nowhere near in the position to take both Rodney and Montez out, so I agreed to tag along. It took us thirty minutes to pull up to some small house in Quincy.

"It's really sad I have to do this shit because when she came to me asking me to hide her out, I made her kick the drugs. She's looking right, and I've been dipping in her honey pot on the regular. I know she's asleep because she takes Tylenol PM around ten every night to help her knock out," Rodney explained as he slipped the key into the lock and opened the door.

Hearing that she finally got her shit halfway together made what was about to go down all the worse, and I hated that I was going to play a role in her baby never seeing her again. Being a parent, I couldn't begin to imagine Lenny having to hear that daddy wasn't coming back ever again. "I'm gonna wait in here while you do what you got to do," I told Rodney.

Ten minutes later, I heard him yell for me to come help him, and when I went in the room, I couldn't believe this sick bastard. He was holding A'Kirah's tongue in one hand and had carved the words, 'You 2 late' across her chest. "Grab her feet and help me put her in the trunk. I'm dropping this hoe off on Laron's doorstep."

Something in my gut was telling me not to fall asleep because, the way Stefon left earlier, I couldn't help but feel like something was wrong, and whatever it was, it wasn't good. Since he returned home a few months ago, things were going so well between us. Slowly but surely, I was finding my heart skipping a beat the way it once had when we first met. Watching Stefon with Lenny was the key part in falling back in love with that man. I only wished he was able to come back and forgive Montez the same way he had me so that we all could move forward peacefully.

My instincts were confirmed when Stefon rushed into the room looking like he seen a ghost. He looked like something heavy was on his mind, and I wasn't going to ask nor push the issue. I knew my baby father, and if anything, he would volunteer up the information on his own and let me know only what I needed to and nothing more. He was pacing back and forth, mumbling under his breath, and I was straining my ears, trying to make out what he was saying, but no matter how hard I tried to tune in, I couldn't make out the words.

Rolling over so I was closer to where Stefon was now standing, I managed to hear, "I done fucked up and got in a little too deep with the devil." He just repeated the same phrase over and over as if it was his favorite tune, and the more he heard the lyrics, the more sense it made. Now, curiosity was getting the best of me, and I wanted to know what the hell he was talking about. As far as I knew, he was doing business with Jervon, and although he wasn't the man I once thought he was, I still couldn't see him as being someone that had Stefon so shook up.

Unable to resist, I decided to speak up. "What could Jervon have done so bad that has you acting like this, Stefon? I've never seen you so on edge."

He stopped short, walked over, and took a seat next to me on the bed, only to hop back up and continue walking the length of the room. "I'm not talking about his ass."

"Well then who, because as far as I know, the only person you have any dealings with is his ass!" I shouted and didn't mean to, but the way he was behaving had me concerned. When you were in that line of work, any wrong move, and the people closest to you could end up paying. I had a son I needed to be worried about, and playing Trivia Pursuit wasn't the way I wanted to get answers.

"Trin, baby, I need you to hear me out and try and understand. I have to leave again for a while. It's the only thing I can do to keep you and Lenny safe." Before I could dig deeper and ask what the hell was going on, Stefon leaned down, gave me a passionate kiss, and walked out the room.

I wasn't about to allow his ass to walk out and not tell me what the hell was going on. And it wasn't even about me wanting to know every detail, specifically who this 'devil' was he kept referencing, but I *needed* to know. How was I supposed to protect me and Lenny if I don't know who to watch out for? And why was I gonna be left alone without his ass making sure we would be safe?

When I reached my son's bedroom door, I stopped short and watched on as Stefon placed a soft kiss on our son's forehead and whispered, "I love you, son, and I don't want you to ever think differently. Daddy is gonna fix this mess, and then we're all leaving this city behind us. Me, you, Mommy, and hopefully give you some siblings to bully."

Stefon turned to face me, and my heart melted. His cheeks were drenched from the tears that were pouring out of his eyes. If I wasn't sure before, I knew without a doubt, right here in this moment that he loved our son. The only other time I had seen him this emotional was the day Lenny decided to finally make his entrance. Stefon was clearly conflicted on what he wanted to do.

Leaving now would throw everything he had built with our son out the window. A baby had such a short attention span, and they didn't have the same capabilities to remember everything. That was why it was so damn important to instill consistency in their lives and brains. It was why Disney and Nick Jr. did repeat shows all week long. The more you saw something and heard something, the more you were able to lock it into your brain.

"You don't have to go," I whispered.

Pulling me from our son's room and into the living room, Stefon wrapped me in his arms. He was hugging me so damn tight I thought he was going to break some ribs. "Can you please talk about me to Lenny every day? Don't let him forget me. God willing, I'm finding a way to make everything better and fix this mess. Everything that's going on isn't because of the beef I have with Montez. This is not my doing, but like a dumbass, I put myself into it, and now I'm involved."

If you asked me, Stefon was talking in riddles. How did he have nothing to do with it but running because he was involved? And what exactly took place? "What happened? What changed?"

"You will find out I'm sure by morning. I love you, Trinity." And just like that, without packing a bag or looking back, I was left alone to play mommy and daddy to a young son. For the first time in a long time, when I got back to my room, I dropped to my knees and prayed. Stefon hadn't always made the right choices, and his need to fit in always landed him in trouble. I just hoped that nothing tragic happened to him because as much as I tried to deny it, I did still love him.

The next morning, the first thing I did was turn on the news to see if I could see anything that would make last night's events make sense, but nothing they were talking about seemed connected to Stefon. I made my way into the bathroom to handle my hygiene before waking my baby up to get him ready to go to Mrs. Williams. I thought I was going to be able to quit the day job at the motel, but now I was relieved I hadn't taken Stefon's advice when he had suggested it.

On the way into work, my phone rang, and it was my sister, Tia, so I answered. "Is it true what they're saying?"

"Is what true?" I asked her.

"Girl, everyone talking about A'Kirah is dead, and Laron is out for blood."

I didn't need to look at myself in a mirror to know that the color had drained from my face hearing that. And I couldn't help but to blame myself for telling Stefon last night what I overheard Montez talking about. As much as I loved my sister, she was what some would call the hood blog because she was always talking up on someone's mess, so I had to choose my response carefully. "Why is he out for blood? Her ass more than likely shot up too much dope."

"That's what I said, when Nay told me she heard from Bre that she was over Laron's house, and when she was leaving, A'Kirah was asleep on the porch. When he went to wake her up, he realized she was dead. But Bre said she was killed and dumped there."

"Killed how? Who the hell would want to kill her ass?" I questioned. I mean, I had some ideas, but I wasn't going to speak on it. Stefon definitely played a major role in her dying. His behavior hours ago said it all.

"I don't know. She probably owed someone money," Tia said.

Instead of going to work, I turned around and headed back home. On the way there, I called Fayth and asked her to come over to talk. I needed to see what she knew about Jervon and who else him and Stefon were dealing with. When I went to call Stefon just to check on him, the phone went right to voicemail. Next, I went to locate phone, and when it showed he was at my house, I got excited, thinking he had a change of mind. But once I arrived, I found it sitting on the side table. He must have left it behind last night. Turning it on, I was hoping that I would find something in it to help me solve shit, but like any other time I looked in his shit, all I found was photos of me and Lenny and nothing more. No texts, calls, emails, or messages of any sort.

## Chapter Ten
## MONTEZ

Man, shit was crazy. Getting that call from Laron this morning was something I didn't really see coming. The cold part about it was he didn't sound too hurt over discovering his baby mama's body on his porch. I knew she wasn't shit once she got on the drugs, but I remembered a time when that man loved the hell out of her ass. That might be the part that seemed so absurd to me. How calm and stoic Laron's tone was when he was telling me how he discovered her.

"Ayo, you good tho'?" I asked while licking my lips, watching sexy ass Fayth get dressed. I had stayed with her at her condo after we left from my granny's birthday.

"I mean, like I said, I knew this day was gonna come, so it ain't nothing. My kid don't really know who she is. What I am worried about is the damn police. I didn't want to call them, but Bre was here last night, and she saw A'Kirah's body. Had they not cut her fucking tongue out and carved no shit in her chest, I would've just made sure she had some dope in her body and called it in. Now I have to deal with why she was left here," Laron stated.

"Well listen, I'm gonna make a few moves real quick and put word on the street that the money I had leading to finding her will double if anyone can provide me with solid evidence of who is responsible for this shit, and don't worry about funeral expenses. This is on me, bruh."

Fayth heard my last comment and asked, "Is everything OK?"

"Yeah. My people were killed last night. It's all part of the game, but I still like to look out and help if I can." I chose to leave out most of the details.

"Well I'm sorry for your loss. I'm about to get ready for work." I guess that was her way of telling me to get the fuck up and go. But I was fine with it because I had some moves to make. Specifically, to go see my cousin. It was time me and Stefon had another talk. I saw his ass leave from granny's party last night, in a rush, and it so happened to be after I got the phone call that A'Kirah was ready to come forward and tell me who had her sneaking around my shit.

Arriving at Trinity's house, I didn't see my bitch ass cousin's car outside, but I did see hers. I knew from back when I was still fucking her that she normally wouldn't be home right now but at work. I chopped it up as maybe they were switching cars for the day, so I went inside the building and up to her door. The second she opened it, I barged inside and could tell she was scared as fuck.

"Where the fuck is Stefon at!" I yelled, storming through her house, looking for my cousin.

"Your guess is as good as mine. He left."

"Where did he go?"

"I don't know. I don't ask that man to run down his every damn move to me. He told me he was leaving, and that was it," Trinity said.

When I looked down, I spotted not one but two phones sitting on the couch. One of them I knew to belong to her, and the other one I saw was opened and on Stefon's snapchat. "Oh, y'all must've knew I was coming. What, his scary ass run down the fire escape?" I yelled.

"I told you he fucking left. I don't know what the hell is going on, Montez, but you need to leave."

"Nah, I'm gonna sit right here until he decides to show his face. You want me to believe that muthafucka left his phone behind and unlocked for a bitch to go through it?" I chuckled because just saying the shit sounded dumb as fuck.

"That's exactly what happened. Listen, I have no idea what's going on, Montez, but I assure you Stefon ain't who you need to be looking for. Tia told me about A'Kirah, and do I think Stefon knows something, yes, but he ain't responsible. That man looked petrified when he came in here last night. He said he's gonna fix everything and left. I shouldn't be telling you all this, but I am. At the end of the day, that's your damn blood, and you know Stefon ain't a killa."

Trinity had no idea who the fuck she laid down and had a baby with, because his ass had a few bodies under him. Granted, they weren't as grim as A'Kirah's, but that didn't mean shit. "Trin, you need to think long and hard about where he is. Get ahold of him somehow and tell him to get at me because shit ain't looking too good for him."

After I got all that out the way and saw that she understood how serious shit was, I looked at her lips, and my dick got hard. I was about to try to talk her out of some head when someone knocked on the door. "Who is it?" Trinity asked.

"Fayth," I heard. The fuck kind of bullshit was going on? I just left from this bitch's house, and she claimed she was getting ready to go to work, not come here.

When she saw me open the door, her eyes got large. "Unbelievable. So, you leave from my bed and come over here to fuck another woman. I'm glad you ain't shit but some revenge dick."

"Fayth, can you come inside. Ain't nobody in here want his ass no more. That's old news," Trinity voiced.

Something wasn't right, and I felt like I was being set up. "I thought you had work?" I asked Fayth.

"I was getting ready to leave my house when Trinity asked me to come here as soon as possible. It sounded like she really needed somebody to talk to, and so I called out. She was there for me after all when I wrecked my car, so I was returning the favor."

I couldn't say I bought all of what Fayth was saying, but

her voice sounded sincere, and I was pretty good at picking up when someone wasn't being truthful. "Fayth, do you have any idea who Stefon and Jervon could be working with?" Trinity asked.

"Huh?" I asked, confused.

"No. Just knowing that Jervon was into something illegal was shocking to me. I don't know who the hell that man is," Fayth said to Trinity then turned to me and said, "What don't you understand?"

"Nothing. Aye, check it out. I need to talk to you so let's go," I told her, heading out the door and stopped so she could see I meant what I said, then I looked at Trinity. "Find my stupid ass cousin and have him get at me."

Fayth did as I had asked and shrugged her shoulders before following me out the building. I got in my car, and she got in hers. I knew I was going to be able to use her for something other than sex. Seeing as my dick was so powerful and had helped me get my way with bitches, I knew it was going to come in handy in figuring out all this mess.

We went inside my house, and as soon as the door was closed and locked, I carried her to my bed. "I just wanted to feel you one more time. Had me standing in that living room, dick all hard," I exaggerated. I mean, it was standing at attention, but originally, it was because I was picturing Trinity's lips wrapped around it. But now I was gonna get some good pussy and make this bitch become my little puppet. I knew she was sprung when she didn't put up a fight and agreed to leave with me.

Removing her sexy ass from the scrubs she was wearing, I knew I was 'bout to taste her sweet nectar before I did anything else. Fayth just had the kind of pussy that drew you to lick it even if you weren't into that shit. After I watched her eyes roll to the back of her head, I grabbed her hand and brought it to my dick. I knew she felt that precum oozing from the head. Without me having to tell Fayth, she moved her pussy away from me and slid onto the floor to her knees, taking my manhood into her mouth. Now it was my turn to have my eyes roll.

Fayth had me ready to tap out, and as much as I wanted to coat her throat, I really wanted to prolong my nut. "Come get on top," I ordered. As she made her way up, she started to kiss on my abs. When she began to suck on my nipple, I almost went upside her head, but once I got over the shock, her warm tongue calmed me down. For a second, she had me questioning myself because this was some gay shit.

"Push back some. I want you to see this pretty ass clap while you fill me up with all that dick you got." I did just as Fayth had requested, and at first, it took her a second to find the right rhythm, but once she got into it, I could barely see my dick because her cheeks were blocking the view.

*Smack! Smack!* I kept taking turns, leaving handprints. I had to give it to Ron, the plastic surgeon I was in business with, because you couldn't tell me that Fayth had no ass just two months ago. Her shit bounced like a bitch from the south that was cornbread fed.

"Fuck, Montez. I'm about to cum!" Fayth moaned out,

sounding out of breath. I knew being on top was a lot of work for her at the moment, seeing as her leg wasn't fully healed.

"Then fucking cum so I can lay you on your back. I know that shit hurts." Instead of slowing up, she went crazy. It was as if the pain was driving her to achieve that orgasm at all costs. Fayth didn't need to tell me she was cumming. Her body told it all as her walls tightened around my dick and she froze in place. The second she loosened the hold she had on me, her juices trailed down onto me.

I tapped her ass, indicating I needed for her to get up. "I can't move, Montez. I'm stuck." Fayth was half laughing, half crying.

"Crazy woman." I laughed with her as I grabbed ahold of her waist and stood up, giving her the assistance she so clearly needed. "Now lay on your side," I instructed now that she was standing on her feet. Well, barely. I could tell that she overdid it, and as much as some would say I was an asshole, I knew Fayth was in pain. But I had something for that.

"Wait one second. Let me grab you something for your pain," I said.

"I have my prescription in my bag. I don't take street drugs," Fayth expressed.

"The fuck you think I was gonna give you? Some dope or something? I don't keep that kind of shit just laying around my damn house," I spat, feeling judged.

"I didn't think that you were going to give me illegal street drugs, but I do see cases where patients have bought pain killers in the street and they aren't real. Can you grab my purse from my car, or should I just leave because now shit seems awkward?"

Without responding, I pulled my sweats up over my waist, grabbed her keys from where she dropped them on my floor, and headed outside to my driveway to grab her bag. When I opened her car door, her phone was flashing with a message from Trinity. Fayth was so damn naïve she didn't have a code on it, so I slid my finger down her screen so I wouldn't have to open up the message and read that Trinity was asking for Jervon's number so she could see if he knew anything Stefon may be involved in.

I stopped in the kitchen to grab a bottle of water for Fayth to take her medicine, and as bad as I wanted to get back to fucking her, I couldn't. My mind kept going to the message and that feeling that these bitches knew exactly what was going on and were playing a part in me being set up. I was never the type of man to sweat anything, but what were the chances that Jervon would start coming to the club on the weekends with Ron around the same time Stefon appeared back in town?

"Thank you," Fayth said when I handed her the Celine handbag.

While she was opening the bottle of pills, I decided to ask her a few questions. At first, I planned on talking to her after I had her dickmatized, but my dick didn't want to work with the thoughts that she could possibly be linked to those trying to take me down. Looking Fayth straight in her eye so I could look for any signs of her lying to me, I asked, "What does

Trinity mean by Stefon and your man having dealings? Is there something I need to know?"

Rolling her eyes, she replied, "We already went through this shit. Whatever Jervon has going on, he kept from me. I thought I was marrying an honest man who dedicated his life to not only me but to his career as a doctor. It wasn't until we went to dinner did I meet Trinity and Stefon and discovered he was supplying pills to Stefon. In his defense, he is only trying to help those that can't afford to see a doctor. Jervon isn't that man you are thinking he is. He's not capable of being a drug lord, but I don't really want to talk about him."

"Does he trust you?" I asked.

Fayth nodded her head and went to say something, but I placed my finger to her lips to hush her up because I wasn't done asking questions, but when she sucked the shit and started to pretend like it was a dick, I lost focus. My man sprung to life, and I found myself pushing my pants down and laying her pretty ass back. The conversation wasn't over. I was gonna have to ask what I needed to while fucking her.

"You like this dick? You like how I make this pussy feel?" I asked while I was leaning down and talking softly into her ear.

"Mhmm," she moaned.

"That's not an answer." I stopped moving and threatened to pull out.

Like I knew she would, Fayth grabbed my hips and pulled me back into her and started to grind on me from beneath me. "Don't stop. Let me feel it." She begged.

"You want this?" I questioned as I pulled out then slammed back in.

"Oh my, yes..." She cried.

"Will you do whatever I ask you to do, and in return, I'll give you this whenever you want it?"

Fayth nodded her head, but I wanted to hear her agree to it. I slid out and held back my laughter when I saw her lips start to pout. "Answer the question, Fayth."

"Yes, Montez, damn. Can you stop teasing me?" When I didn't do what she wanted, her hand went down, and she started to finger bang herself. Fayth reached for my dick with her other hand and tried to insert it. Smacking her hand, I gave her what she wanted.

I continued to please Fayth until I knew she couldn't take another orgasm. I had her right where I needed her to be, so I pounded until I released. Fuck! I thought to myself when I pulled out and realized I was bareback. My stupid ass slipped up and nutted in this bitch because I wasn't focused on anything but making sure Fayth would agree to work with me.

"I need you to do me a favor," I said, lying down next to Fayth.

"Mm hmm," she replied. When I looked over, her eyes were closed, and I knew she was about to pass out.

"I need you to come work for me at Diamonds but not as a dancer. You sexy as fuck, but baby, you got no rhythm."

What I said grabbed her attention, and her head snapped back, and her face wore a frown. It was cute. "Wow."

"Don't look at me like that. You too special to me for me

to allow you to shake your ass for all them men. I need for you to work VIP as a bottle girl. Specifically, the nights when Ron and your ex are in attendance. I need you to get in his head and see who he's working with. Lives are being claimed, and I know you don't want Trinity to be another casualty," I said, laying it on thick.

"I don't know what you think I can find out, but I'll try. I don't want anyone to get hurt. Not even Jervon, and I'm certain that whatever is going on, he has nothing to do with it. He's not like that."

"All I ask is you to try to find out what you can. And in return, you can get this whenever and wherever you want!" I expressed while grabbing ahold of my semi-hard dick and shaking it for her to see.

## Chapter Eleven
# JERVON

I had handled my business for the day, and it was time for me to head over to Diamonds to unwind. Not to mention, I was hoping to run into Trinity and see if she'd tell me what was going on with Stefon. I'd been trying to reach him for just about a week now, and to no prevail, which was odd. He practically begged me to get my hands on more pills, and I was finally able to get another rep from a different pharmaceutical company to do business with me. I just had to pray that Shawnda didn't find out. Not only were the two agencies in competition with each other, but Shawnda and Mary also competed.

As soon as I walked inside of Diamonds and headed toward VIP, I couldn't believe my eyes. It was like my feet became lead and wouldn't move. Standing in front of Ron was my girl, half naked. She was pouring him a drink and showing off my body that I paid for. Granted, he was the one who created it, but it was meant to be mine. Wasn't this about a bitch?

It was the first time I'd seen Fayth since they put her in the ambulance, and I missed the hell out of her. I fucked up by messing shit up, but it really wasn't my fault. It was the dumb bitch at the hospital that couldn't take no for an answer and had me fired. If I still had that job, then I never would've been into all the other shit that followed. There would be no Stefon, no Shawnda, and now no Mary. I would never understand how someone balanced different females, because it was too much work.

I wanted to run up on Fayth and mush her in her damn face before knocking my so-called best friend the fuck out. "You got to be kidding me! I knew this shit would happen. I told you I didn't want Ron to see you naked because he would want to fuck you once he saw how pretty your pussy was." I started to go off on Fayth the second I entered the closed off area.

"Boy, please." She laughed at the same time Ron chuckled. They thought shit was funny, but I was about to show them how hilarious I could get. "I ain't that type of bitch. I'm working. Nothing more. Nothing less."

Ron felt the need to add his two cents as well. "As much pussy as I see on the table every week, trust and believe, Fayth don't have the prettiest. And I mean that in the least disrespectful way. It's fucked up you would even think I'd do some disloyal shit like that to you, bro. I thought we were better than that."

That all sounded good, and I was sure was the truth, but out of all the places she could work, why here? I needed to hear her explanation, because Fayth wasn't even this type of female to be strutting around leaving little to the imagination. "Why here? And why do you feel the need to get a second job, Fayth? I hope you ain't trying to get more surgery done." That was the only thing I could come up with, thinking back to when she was working at the gas station to pay for her ass to be done.

"Because I need a damn car, and I have bills I have to pay on my own, so I need easy money."

I reached for her hand, but she pulled away from me. Fayth didn't need to be working in a damn club. Not when she had a man who loved her the way I did. "Can we step outside and talk please?"

Surprisingly, she agreed, and placed the bottle of Patrón she had in her hand down and started walking in the opposite direction of the door. "It's too cold to be outside with nothing on. We can talk in the employee bathroom."

"Fayth, let me come back home and help you with bills. This isn't the life you dreamed of living," I stated as soon as we stepped into the restroom.

"I can't do that. Yes, I forgive you for all you have done because I needed to for my own piece of mind, but it's not so easy to forget all the lies you fed me. You were basically fired from the hospital but had me believing that you were still working there, yet you was living part time with another woman. Do you hear how that sounds?" She cried, and I felt horrible.

"I can admit I went about things the wrong way, but I didn't want to let you down, and I knew coming home and telling you that some of the women at the hospital falsely accused me of trying to sleep with them, you would question me. It might be hard to believe given everything else, but I swear to you, I never did that. Not once. That same night, I bumped into Stefon, and when he let me know how much money was to be made from selling pills, I thought about us. The wedding of your dreams. The big house we always talked about filled with kids. So, I went to Shawnda to see if she could help me. I never meant for things to get out of hand," I explained.

"Is that supposed to make me feel better, Jervon? You're basically saying you got involved with another woman for me? Yet you stopped putting money into the joint account, became a regular at a strip club, and Lord knows what other secrets have yet to be discovered. Nah! Everything you did, are doing, and will do, was all for your own selfish needs. But as I said a minute ago. I forgive you because hating you is impossible."

I took both of her hands into mind and looked Fayth dead in her eyes. "At least let me try to make things right. Don't throw everything we built and all the good times away without putting up a fight," I begged.

After a few moments of silence, she nodded her head but

added, "You still can't come home, and we're not together. You have a lot to prove, and I want to know everything you have going on. No more secrets, Jervon."

"Thank you, baby," I said, leaning in to give her a kiss, but she curved the hell out of me. "How are you getting home?"

"Lyft. The same way I been getting around," Fayth answered.

"Wrong. Let me drive you to the house." Again, she nodded then headed toward the door to leave. Seeing as I was still holding her hand, I pulled her back and hugged her tightly. She felt so damn good in my arms. This was home, and I had to figure out a way to get things back to normal because the only woman I wanted to have my last name was the one before me. There was no doubt in my mind.

For the remainder of the night, I sat back and was on my best behavior as I watched Fayth prance around in boy shorts and pasties, pouring drinks. Every time she bent over to hear what someone was saying to her, her shorts dug deeper into her ass, and I was both turned on and pissed off. Nobody but me was supposed to benefit from her little operation, but here we were, and a whole club was viewing what was mine. I knew I was in no position to make any demands, but in due time, this job would just be another thing of her past. I wasn't going to sit back and allow this little gig to carry on. I just needed to get things right between us first.

The ride back to my old residence was an awkward one. It was after two in the damn morning, and Fayth had her face planted in her phone, texting back and forth with someone.

When I tried to look over, she partially turned her body facing me, to block me from seeing her screen. In all the years we were together, she was never a phone person, because she didn't have anyone to really talk with. "Who got you so occupied that you can't talk to me?" I finally asked.

"A friend," she replied simply.

"And who might that be, Fayth? You don't have friends."

She laughed and put her phone down. "Things have changed, Jervon. I have plenty of friends now."

I didn't know how to feel about that. Part of me felt like she was trying to be rebellious because of the events surrounding my infidelity, but then another part of me felt like it had to do with her new body. Something I was now kicking myself in the ass for not only agreeing to but paying for. Even the outfit she had on right now just to ride home in was something Fayth would've never put on before. It was fall here in Boston, and I could see the bottom half of her tits because the shirt she was wearing was so damn small.

"You wanna come up?" Fayth asked when I pulled up in front of the building. I wasn't planning on staying because, quite frankly, I didn't think she would be down with it, but what I wasn't going to do was deny the opportunity to spend some much-needed time with Fayth.

"Sure. I'm gonna park in your spot and not out here on the street." The last thing I needed was for Shawnda to decide to look for me and stumble across my car out in the open and know that I was with Fayth. When I had my mail forwarded to her house, the stupid ass post office sent a change of address confirmation letter to Shawnda's house, and she opened it. She now knew where I was living with Fayth, and when I didn't walk in the house, I knew this would be her first place to look.

The good thing about the building me and Fayth had a condo in was the garage residents parked in was secured. In order to access the area that was underneath the building, you needed to have a security code.

"That's fine. Like I said, back in Diamonds when you thought I was there to fuck your friend, I am working on buying a new car. I don't want to lease or finance one. I want to make enough money to buy one outright," Fayth explained, which she didn't need to.

As soon as we walked in the front door, my heart sank. Every photograph that once adorned the walls of me and Fayth were no longer up. The apartment even smelled different. The hint of my cologne that once lingered could no longer be smelled. "Damn, you just erased any sign of me from in here."

"I had to. It hurt too much. I washed every piece of material that I could and hired a cleaning company to do the furniture and walls. If only there was a service I could've hired to erase every trace of you from my heart, but unfortunately, only time will help that."

"So, you don't want to love me anymore?" I questioned as I stepped into her personal space.

I could see Fayth's breathing become shallow. I knew her

heart was racing because mine started to, and our hearts were always in sync. "Why should I?"

"Because, despite how shit looks or what you think, I love you, Fayth. I don't want to live without you. I got in too deep and got caught up in a life that ain't for me, but I'm in too deep right now to just walk away. It's gonna take some time to figure out a safe way, but for you, I will."

Fayth reached up and wrapped her arms around my neck and kissed me. Next thing I knew, Fayth was leaned over the back of the sofa while I was letting off my first nut of the night. I had missed being inside of Fayth so much that I couldn't help but to cum prematurely. "Let's go to the bedroom. As much as I appreciated that, I'm still hungry for more," I suggested, and thankfully, she didn't object.

The other area of the house may not have smelled like anything but apples, but in the room, I was almost certain I could pick up on the scent of a man. But there was no way that could be what it was. Fayth probably used one of those masculine candles she claimed she didn't like that my parents gifted us last Christmas.

"Baby, I want you to ride me," I said while I was removing my clothes seeing as neither of us had gotten fully undressed.

"I can't. My leg isn't fully healed. I think I caused more damage when I cut the cast off before it was due to be removed," Fayth replied. I wanted to ask her why she would do something so careless, but the last thing I wanted to do was waste time going back and forth over something that had been done, when I wanted us to go back and forth and trade an orgasm for a nut.

For the remainder of the night and up until the early morning, we explored each other's bodies like it was our first time. And in a sense, it was, because the animal that Fayth had become between the sheets was someone I didn't know. Maybe it was because she possessed more confidence with her new body, but whatever the reason was, I wasn't mad.

When we finally had enough, Fayth was laying with her head on my chest. "Jervon, if this is going to work, I need to know everything you have going on. I don't want any more secrets to pop up."

"What exactly do you want to know? You already know what dealings I have with Stefon. And you now know about who I get the pills from and what I have to do to keep getting them."

She lifted her head slightly to look at me. "I can't help the gut feeling like there's more people involved. Who else are the two of you doing business with? Trinity told me that someone died the other day, and she's connected to Stefon somehow."

That was the first I had heard of anyone dying, but it could explain why I hadn't heard from Stefon in a few days. "That's the first I've heard of it, and if Stefon is involved, then you just told me something he should've. All I can tell you is I get the pills and hand them off to him. We meet up whenever he needs more or for him to give me my cut. Whoever he's working with to help sell them is a mystery."

I wasn't lying. I genuinely had no idea who else may be involved in the business I was doing with Stefon. To me, it didn't matter. But now it had me thinking. I needed to know all sides of this little business so I didn't get dragged into something I had no idea about. "I hate that I had introduced you to Stefon and Trinity that night. Now you can be connected to what's going on, and I don't like that. I'm sorry."

She dropped her head back to my chest and said nothing more. As bad as I wanted to just stay here and cuddle with Fayth, I knew I couldn't. Unfortunately, the double life I was living wasn't something of my past. I still had Shawnda that I had to go home to. "Umm, Fayth. Please don't get upset, but I ummm, have to..." I started to say when she pulled away from me.

"I already know what you're going to say, and it's okay. I know you have to leave. I'm not upset. I actually need to get a few hours of sleep in because I have plans in a few hours."

That wasn't the response I was expecting. It kinda bothered me to see her as calm as she was. I pulled her body on top of mine, pushed the few pieces of hair that was in her face to the side, and pecked her lips. "I'm going to make things right. If it's the last thing I do. We will get back to where we once were, and we will be husband and wife. I don't love her, Fayth. I never did, and I never will. It's just business."

"I told you I understand," Fayth replied.

"Baby, I don't want you to be upset and change your mind about us rebuilding."

Fayth sat all the way up, but instead of looking at me, she

looked at the wall. "I told you I fucking understand, Jervon. Now go home to her before I do get mad."

Not wanting to upset Fayth more than I already had, despite her claims that she was unbothered, I slid out the bed and quietly got dressed. Before I walked out the door, I attempted to give her a kiss, but she turned her face, resulting my lips to land on her cheek. "You will get that privilege once you become solely mine. Yes, I pecked your lips a few times tonight, but I will not lock lips with you until you are all mine."

I had to respect what Fayth was saying. But I also knew I couldn't do anything other than that. My ass was lucky she was just willing to fuck with me. Right now, I'd take whatever it was that I could from her. Without so much as taking a piss, I left out the condo and headed to Shawnda's.

The whole way home, I said a prayer that Shawnda would still be asleep, because I was too exhausted to deal with the line of questions that I was sure she was going to burden me with. But I should've known that the big man above wasn't rocking with me lately with all the sinning I'd been doing, so I was greeted with the opposite of my prayers. Shawnda was waiting up in the bed with a stern look on her face.

When she didn't say anything, I thought maybe I was in the clear, so I went over to my dresser to get out some under-clothes to take a shower. I was regretting not at least washing my dick off before I left Fayth's, but I wasn't thinking about Shawnda and getting caught. My mind was just happy that Fayth was fucking with my ass again.

"Where the hell were you? And don't try lying!"

"Ron got too fucked up, so I drove him home in my car. He passed out on the way there, so I had to basically carry his heavy ass in the house. I didn't want to leave him alone in the event he suffered from alcohol poisoning, so I stayed there, watching him, to make sure he didn't suffocate in his own vomit." I couldn't believe how easy that lie fell from my lips.

"You could've called me. I was worried and called around to all the hospitals and police stations."

"You're right, and I'm sorry. I'm hungry, sore, and tired. Do you think you can order something to be delivered for breakfast? I'd ask you to cook but you look just as tired," I asked, getting ready to go to the bathroom and shower. "I'm gonna hop in a shower. I smell like liquor and vomit."

"Okay. I'll see what place is delivering right now from UberEATS," Shawnda replied.

I couldn't believe my luck. I just knew she was going to fight and argue. I stripped out of my clothes and stepped into the large shower that could fit at least five grown adults. My mind started replaying everything that took place tonight, and my dick started to get hard thinking about the way Fayth felt. "She must have really loved the way you were dicking her down," I heard Shawnda say.

"What the fuck you talking about?" I questioned.

"Besides the fact that your eyes are closed and you were so deep in thought you didn't hear me asking you what you wanted from Denny's, your dick is hard, and don't try lying about where you were either; the hoe left a bite mark on your shoulder," Shawnda said.

"Shawnda, I wasn't with no damn bitch, so stop accusing me. I told your ass that Ron was drunk off his ass. While I was trying to hold him up and bring him into his house, he fucking bit down on me as he tripped. Why do you want to think the worse of me?" Another quick lie and I was proud of myself. I knew if someone was to tell me these lines, then I'd believe them. They sounded that believable.

"Don't let me find out you playing me, Jervon. I'm warning you."

A chill went up my spine, and my once semi-hard dick went back into its shell. The way Shawnda said that confirmed that I didn't know who I was in bed with. Her ass sounded like a completely different person and one that I knew I didn't want no dealings with.

## Chapter Twelve
# FAYTH

I couldn't wait for Jervon to hurry the hell up and leave so I could run to the pharmacy and not only pick up my refill for pain meds but to buy a Plan B pill. Here I was, sleeping with two men, all within the same week, without protection, and the last thing I needed was a baby and not know for certain who the daddy was. I had no intentions of even taking it there with Jervon's dirty dick ass, but when Montez sent me a text after I left from Diamonds, telling me to do what I had to do to get him the information he needed, I knew that would mean sleeping with Jervon.

My fear was once I went there with Jervon, that old feelings I was trying so hard to forget would rush back to the forefront. And surprisingly, they didn't. I didn't feel nothing more than I had before I made the decision to help Montez. I recalled a time when I lived and breathed everything Jervon.

And that little detail was what hurt me. It also let me know that, once I got from him everything that Montez wanted to know, I was definitely cutting all lines of communication with him again. The love just wasn't there anymore. We weren't the same no more.

Once I showered and slipped on a pair of jeans and a nice fitted shirt, I took in my appearance and smiled. Long gone were the days of snapping mirror flicks and deleting because there was nothing to look at. Now I found myself uploading at least five pictures at a time because I couldn't decide which one I liked the most. Never mind the hundreds of followers I gained, mainly men, who all loved everything I posted.

Happy with how I looked, as simple as my attire was, I headed out the door to go handle what I needed to. Just as I was stepping out my building to look for my Lyft, Montez sent me a ten second video of him stroking his dick and told me if I wanted to catch his load to hurry up. All I could think about was feeling the perfectly shaped beast gave me, so instead of going to CVS, I headed right to his house, for an extra fee of course, seeing as my original destination was for the pharmacy. I still had two pain pills, so I could wait until later in the night to go grab my prescription and the Plan B.

I didn't think I got out of the car so fast in my life as I did when I pulled into Montez's driveway, calling his phone on the way to the door so he knew I had arrived. All the while, I was praying I wasn't too late. For a second, I felt like a damn addict, but for something entirely different than what the government labeled as narcotics. However, the dick down that Montez delivered always left me feeling high and tingly and anxious for the next time I would be blessed with it.

"Oh shit," Montez said, picking up the phone.

"I'm at your door. Hold it, baby. I'm coming in," I said.

Before I could turn the knob, the door opened, and this asshole was standing there with a smirk on his sexy ass face and fully dressed. I guess he could see the confusion mixed with disappointment on my face and laughed. "Relax. I sent you an old video, and it's nothing for me to get hard. I didn't think you would really rush over here."

"Fuck you!" I spat, really in my feelings. I had shit to do, even if one of the things on that list did consist of seeing Montez. It was just later in the day after I did everything else.

"Oh, you really mad, but standing there ain't gonna get you no dick, unless of course you don't mind the neighbors being creeps and watching us."

He didn't have to say nothing more. I was in the house with a big Kool-Aid smile on my face. Montez closed the door behind me and went and sat on the couch. I thought we were going to go right to the bedroom, but I wasn't going to embarrass myself more than I already had, so I took a seat on the opposite chair. If Montez wanted some pussy, he was gonna have to come to me. I was no longer chasing after him. Even if that was what I wanted to do.

"How did your night go?" he inquired.

"Not as planned. He didn't really offer up any new information. Only what I already knew. He provides the pills to Stefon and that's all. The rest of the night went to him begging me to forgive him and talking up a future he wants with me," I told Montez.

"Did he fuck?" Montez asked me.

I wasn't sure if I wanted to tell him the truth, because then it might stop him from wanting to have sex with me now. But what I did know about Montez was he could read people well, and lying wasn't a good way to gain his respect. "Yeah, but only because you said for me to do whatever it took to get him to talk. By taking it there, I realized that the love I once had for him is gone."

Montez appeared to be thinking, then he told me to give him my phone. I wasn't sure what he wanted with it, but curiosity got the best of me. I went to get it from my handbag and handed it over to him. "I can't believe you don't have a damn password on your shit."

"Why would I? I don't got anything to hide."

"You right, but let me delete my damn video. I don't need you losing your phone and some gay muthafucka find it and beat his shit to mine." From where I was sitting, I could tell he was doing more than just removing his video.

"What are you doing?" I asked after seeing him text back and forth with someone.

"I hit up your man and asked him where Stefon is. According to his message back, he is looking for him too and is mad because he has a bunch of pills he needs him to get off. Now I'm trying to tell him to meet up with your friend, me, who will be able to help. He now wants to know what's really going on with us. I'm gonna tell him the truth. I'm your boss."

Hearing Montez say I was just someone working for him upset me. Here I was, getting myself in what appeared to be some drama on a dangerous level because I thought I was something to him, and I wasn't shit. "Fix your face. You know I fuck with you, and I'm not lying to the man. You do work for me, but if I say you're fucking me, then he won't agree to do business with me or give you any information." I guess what he said made sense, and it did make me feel better. "Oh, and he is gonna be staying with you again."

"Wait, what did you just say?" I asked, because surely, I had heard wrong.

"He said he missed you and wanted to come back home. How last night showed him how much he fucked up, followed by a bunch of other lyrics to a sad love song. I told him OK."

"Why would you do that? I don't want him in my space. I just told you I don't feel what I once did for Jervon, and with him there, I won't be able to see you as much," I complained.

Montez moved to where I was, and in the blink of an eye, my shirt was pulled over my head. He was attacking my nipples with his mouth, going from sucking to biting each one as he fumbled with my pants to unbuckle them. Everything he had just told me was forgotten just that quick, and all I could think about was how something as simple as foreplay had my mind spinning. How was this even possible?

"It doesn't matter if y'all live together. I'm still gonna be all up in your pussy, Fayth, and then send you home to his ass. He was doing that with you, and I'm gonna help you get your revenge by doing it right back to him. Tell him you working, and you can be riding my dick."

I didn't think of that, and the wheels started to spin in my head. Jervon being back at the house would mean that he would be back paying half the bills, and I could get me a new car. Montez was a damn mastermind, and I wanted to thank him in a way I knew he would love, by giving him what I learned is called sloppy toppy. I'm not saying I never sucked Jervon's dick and was bad at it. I just thought it was called a blowjob. But when Montez wrapped his hands in my hair and told me to give him that sloppy toppy, I learned another name.

It didn't take long for me to feel Montez coat the back of my throat with his cum. "Fuck, Fayth. You might have the deepest, wettest throat I've ever fucked. Ain't no bitch been able to get me to nut that fast off sucking my dick alone."

I wasn't sure if I should smile or be mad that he was comparing me to other women. Women that I was sure he still dealt with, seeing as we haven't made what we were doing official. Montez started to finger fuck me while sucking on my pearl tongue, and when he stopped and asked if I was going to be his good little bitch and treat Jervon like a king so that he would cooperate, my no turned into a yes. There was no way I wasn't going to agree and risk having him stop attacking my pussy the way he was.

For the next five hours, I hung out with Montez, allowing him to do whatever he pleased to my body. Whatever hole he decided to stick his dick in next, I went with it. We were about to go for another round when my phone went off with Jervon letting me know he was on the way to the condo. I didn't want to leave, but I also didn't want Montez to cut me off from getting any of his dick in the future, so I washed up quickly in his shower and headed to my house. My non-acting ass was about to put on the show of my lifetime.

Five minutes as I arrived back to the house, Jervon was walking in, carrying only a duffel bag. I knew it was the one he kept in his trunk for when he would leave work and want to change from his suit. "What's with the bag? Where's your stuff?"

"Still at Shawnda's house. I can't just go there and pack everything up and leave. She holds too much power and knowledge of the shit I got going on. I'm gonna have to bring things here bit by bit in the bag."

I didn't really much care, and I was relieved he wasn't here with all his shit. I understood where he was coming from though, because from the sounds of it, she could ruin his life. I knew how spiteful women could be because I was one myself, and that's just what I was doing now. His stupid ass was too blind to see that I was getting my payback. He was so worried about trying to not let his girl act out on revenge when I had him caught all up in my spider web. His girl was just making when I kicked his ass out, all the more easy for the two of us when he was no longer useful to what Montez was trying to achieve.

*Chapter Thirteen*

# TRINITY

It'd been over a week since Stefon up and left again, and needless to say, I hadn't been sleeping well. Most nights were spent tossing and turning while wondering where he was and when things would go back to normal. Outside of that, life has been the same. Wake up, shower, get Lenny ready, drop him off, go to the motel, get off work, get Lenny, cook and feed him, give him a bath and get settled while waiting for my sister to come watch him, then hit Diamonds.

Hearing my alarm go off, I groaned because I swore I just closed my eyes, and more than likely, I had, but duty called, and it was time for me to be the responsible adult that I was and get the hell up. Walking into the kitchen to make a much-needed cup of coffee, I knew today was not going to be good. No more K-Cups which meant no java to give me the morning energy I so desperately need. I swore I had an unopened box in the pantry, but the shelves were looking mighty bare. Luckily, there was a can of Coke in the fridge that would have to do until I left and grabbed a coffee from Dunkin Donuts.

If that wasn't bad enough, I realized I hadn't gone grocery shopping, and I had no cereal, no eggs, basically nothing for Lenny to have before I dropped him off at Mrs. Williams. Dragging my ass, I hopped in a quick shower because I now had to leave earlier than I normally did so I could take my baby to get something to eat. I made a mental note to ask Tia what she'd been eating at night while I was at the club, because I couldn't recall a time I didn't have shit to eat in here like I did right now. I knew for a fact I had eggs left over yesterday because I made some for Lenny, seeing as it was his favorite thing to eat.

With the both of us now dressed, I carried him out to my car and strapped him in his big boy car seat. It was crazy how fast my baby was growing. It felt like just yesterday I was able to carry both him and the infant seat down the stairs and click into the base. Those days are long gone, and I was sure, in no time, he would be needing a booster seat. I still had a good year or so before that time hit though. The weather was brisk, which was normal for this time of year in Boston, and it was time to let the car warm up before just pulling off. I hated living in such a rough area because I'd love to be able to just hit the start button from inside the house and enter a nice and toasty vehicle, but with my luck, if I did that here, I'd come outside to no car because some bum would steal it.

I got to McDonald's in no time, and the drive-thru looked ridiculous. Knowing I didn't really have time to wait or I would be late for work, I figured going inside would be my best option. I'd never been the type that was so lazy I would rather spend twenty minutes in my car than walk my ass inside a store and be on my way in half the time. I entered the restaurant and ordered me and my baby something to eat.

As I was carrying our food and holding his hand while he walked slowly beside me, I couldn't help but notice the van parked too close to my car for comfort. There'd been way too many reports of folks being kidnapped for me to fuck around and put my baby at risk. I was getting ready to walk back inside McDonalds when I heard my baby father's voice. "Man, get yo' scary ass in the damn van before you got these people calling the police thinking I'm part of some sick human trafficking ring."

"Da-da!" Lenny yelled, looking around, trying to spot his father.

I wanted to be pissed off, but I couldn't be. The fact that Stefon was deeply involved in a homicide yet he was here making sure that our son didn't forget who he was, warmed my heart. When I got inside the passenger side, prepared to just have a few words with Stefon, he pointed toward the back where there were a few rows of seats. One of which had a car seat. "I don't have much time. I have to get Lenny to Mrs. Williams then head to work. Wait, how did you even know where to find me?" I asked, now realizing that I typically never come to McDonald's for anything, not even a quick bite to eat if it was just me. In my opinion, their burgers were too greasy and upset my stomach.

"You're not going today, and before you get to yelling, I already called them and said you caught a virus," said Stefon.

I climbed over the front seat and strapped Lenny into the seat before taking a seat next to him. Feeding my baby was my first priority, and that meant I couldn't sit way in the front out of arms' reach with Stefon. "Where are we going?"

"To Bellingham. I've been hiding out there with someone I met awhile back. They went away on a business trip for a few days, so I took their church van and came to grab my family to spend some time with me." Fuck everything else he explained. I needed to know where the hell this place was at, because in all my years of living, I had never heard of the place.

"Wait! Hold on, Stefon. Where is that at? And I can't leave for a few days. I don't have any of mine or Lenny's things," I said as Stefon pulled onto the expressway heading south.

"Near Gillette Stadium. Some little town filled with white folk. We can stop off at a Walmart or some place and grab him a few toys and some pullups. I am bringing y'all back tomorrow."

"How do you know I don't have to work at Diamonds tonight?" I asked because I knew he didn't take it upon himself to call Montez and tell him I wouldn't be there.

"You weren't on the schedule. That's why I took it upon myself to have Tia throw away food in the house. I knew you wouldn't send Lenny to Mrs. Williams without feeding him. You'd never hear the end of it if you had. What I didn't know was where you would take him, so I had to follow you here." Whew, Stefon said a mouthful and nothing all at the same time. To know that he went through so much trouble just to spend time with me and our son brought on a warm feeling in my heart and a wet one in my panties.

We drove on the highway for about an hour before he finally took an exit off of 95 South. As soon as we got off, I could see the Walmart sign. Lenny was knocked out and drooling, and I really didn't want to wake my baby up. "I'm gonna run in and grab some things. He's asleep, so you stay in here with him," I told Stefon. I could've easily stayed in the van and had him go inside, but I wanted to get a feel for this little town.

My dream was to always move out of the city to some-place quiet. I just never knew where that would be. This would be the perfect opportunity for me to get a first impression of Bellingham. And I had to admit, I wasn't completely turned off from the treatment I received being a young black girl. An occasional frowned faces, but I wasn't being followed by loss prevention like I had expected. With a small pack of pullups, wipes, pajamas, and a few trucks, I pushed my shopping cart to the woman's section to get a change of panties. They had that little $2.50 section and then their leggings and t-shirts were mad cheap. I went to call Stefon to ask him should I grab snacks and such for Lenny, and I remembered that I had his phone with me that he left behind. Thinking it was better to be safe than sorry, I grabbed some fruit snacks for me and crackers for Lenny, among some other things.

When I made it to the checkout, I was impressed to see that the lines weren't long at all, and I had to laugh. Only in a small town like this would it not look like rush hour traffic at Walmart. Yeah, I could definitely get use to this kind of shopping experience. Or so I thought. It wasn't until it was time to pay and I pulled out my wallet and grabbed my bank card to pay did I get ticked off.

"Will you be using your EBT today?" the cashier questioned.

I had to bite the inside of my cheek to keep myself from cursing this raggedy-senile bitch out, because I was raised better, and if my granny heard me cussing my elder, she'd be on my ass, literally. "You know what. I think I'll pass all together. You can cancel this order, and I'll drive to another store and spend my hard earn money there," I said, while revealing that in my hand wasn't a government issued card with state funded benefits but my actual bank card.

As I was nearing the exit, empty handed, a tall white gentleman wearing a yellow store vest stopped me. "Ma'am, was there a problem?"

"Yes, there was. It's called racial profiling. Your employee assumed I would be paying with food stamps. Now had she asked the woman that was in line before me who actually did use an EBT card but was Caucasian, then I wouldn't think nothing of it. But because the color of my skin is black, she assumed I wasn't paying with debit, cash, or a credit card for that matter."

"I am so sorry for the negative experience you endured. I will be writing her up and letting the general manager know. If you would still like to purchase the items in your cart, I'll be happy to ring you up personally and apply a 10 percent discount off the total."

For a second, I contemplated still leaving without what I had initially came for, but I really didn't feel like finding another store in an area I knew nothing about, so I took him up on the offer. "What took you so long, and what is all this shit?" Stefon asked when I made it back to the van.

"Things I feel like we may need for the night and something to put on for sleep and tomorrow. Soap and snacks. Did you want us to wear the same undergarments? Now had you hit me up and told me about this, then I would've packed me and our son a bag and been willing to even drive out here to you. But that's neither here nor there. I just want to get to this place you've been staying at and get comfortable."

Not even ten minutes later, Stefon was pulling into a driveway that belonged to a cute little yellow house. The street was tree lined, and you could tell that kids was just let outside in their yards to play without the parents sitting with them. This was the kind of neighborhood I always prayed I grew up in and one I wanted for my kids. But if the residents were anything like the lady back in Walmart, I'd have to pass on living my dream. There was no way I'd be able to deal with that bullshit on a regular basis without catching a record.

The interior of the house was cute. A little dated, but definitely an upgrade from the standard city apartment I'd been accustomed to living in. "The décor is cute. A little too country for my taste, but it's homey. Is your 'friend' white?" I asked Stefon while putting my son down on his feet after removing his shoes.

Stefon laughed. "He isn't, but his wife is. You heard of Mike-Mike from Mission?"

The name sounded familiar. "I think I heard some stories about him from one of my cousins. I think she used to mess with him. Was he one of the dudes that got caught up in that big raids the feds did back in the '90s? Folks were calling it Boston's version of the whole Rich Porter case."

"Yeah, that's him. He did his time and got out like two years ago. He met his wife while he was locked down, and when he was released, he moved here with her. My mother used to fuck with one of his uncles, and I reached out, looking for help with this mess going on. He offered for me to come here on the strength that he always liked my mother as an aunt." he explained.

For the next two hours, Stefon played with Lenny on the floor with the cars while I sat back and watched. I was starting to get hungry, so I went to see what was in the house to cook. I knew once Lenny ate something, he'd be ready for another nap, and that would give me and Stefon some time alone. The first sign of my son getting sleepy, I asked Stefon where I should lay him down, and he showed me to a room in the back that had nothing but a big bed in the center and nothing else. No photos, no side table, no television. Just a bed. I knew getting Lenny to conk out without watching *Paw Patrol* was going to be impossible if I didn't lie with him, so I climbed on the bed.

I didn't know who fell asleep first, but next thing I knew, Stefon was lightly shaking me and motioning for me to follow him. No sooner did I get in the hallway did he pick me up and carry me into another room. I knew this was where Stefon actually slept because his scent was all over the bedding. A smell I had started to miss and hadn't realized until this very moment how much.

"I've missed you so damn much, Trin. My dick hurts just looking at you. It wants to feel the comforts of home, and that's always been inside your warm, wet cave."

"Then come on home and let me take away that pain," I said while reaching out to unbuckle his jeans. There was no foreplay. We got right down to business, and the second the head of his dick was inside, I moaned. "Mmm. I missed this feeling."

Prior to me and Stefon's breakup a year ago, he wasn't bad in bed, but Montez was better. There was no denying that. I wasn't sure if I'd just grown as a woman or the time away made me appreciate the man I had, but sex with Stefon became everything to me. The desire to be with anyone else faded. The dreams of being with some successful doctor or lawyer no longer was what I wanted. I had who was made for me all along, and there was no letting what we have go.

With both of my legs cuffed in his forearms, Stefon leaned

forward and kissed my lips, all the while he was moving in and out of me. "Marry me," he whispered against my lips.

I opened my eyes to see if he was serious or was I hearing shit. "What did you just say?"

Stefon raised up some, and with eyes full of lust and love, he repeated what he said. "Marry me, Trinity. I know we've been through some shit that should've broken us and filled our hearts with hate for the other, but it didn't. I've never loved or wanted anyone the way I do when it comes to you. I couldn't cheat on you if I wanted to, because my dick doesn't want to be anywhere else but inside of you."

Nodding my head, I answered the life changing question. "I love you too, Stefon, and of course I want to marry you, but I'm gonna need for you to ask me this question with a clear mind. You always said you were against marriage and it was just a legal piece of paper that didn't determine love."

"That was before I knew what it was like living without you. Feeling the void of you not being mine is something I never want to experience again. Neither of us are perfect. We both have some shit with us, and our pasts are fucked up, but together, we are imperfectly perfect, if that's even a thing," Stefon expressed while never missing a beat as he made love to me.

I had to agree with what he said. We had made mistakes in our lives, some of which I wasn't proud I made, and I was sure he wished he could take back the ones he had. But I guess all that matters now was learning to fully forgive the other, leaving those bad decisions in the past, and moving forward. There was only one thing I was going to need for him to do beforehand: fix things with Montez. Because, at the end of the day, they were blood and were thick as thieves before I got between them. If he could forgive me, then he needed to forgive his cousin as well. Being at odds was not the way to be. Once upon a time when the topic of marriage would come up, Stefon always expressed that wasn't no other man gonna stand beside him at the altar than Montez, and I hated that as things stood right now, that wouldn't happen. In order for his vision to be possible, I knew I was gonna have to step in and do whatever it took to make it happen. But how?

## Chapter Fourteen

# STEFON

When I pulled up to McDonald's to drop Trinity and Lenny off, I couldn't believe my eyes. This bitch had done set me up. If it wasn't for my son being in the car and the fact that she was his mother, I probably would've pulled my gun out and shot her in the fucking face. But instead, I parked beside her car like it wasn't nothing. Something told me on the drive back to Boston that Trinity was being sneaky because she was oddly quiet and kept texting with someone every twenty or so minutes. She must've been updating this muthafucka on where we were at and when we should be back.

While Trinity was getting Lenny from the car seat, Montez jumped in the passenger side seat, and before he could get to talking, I stopped him in his tracks. "Aye, listen. I don't know what the fuck you want or why you even wasting both of our time on being here. Do whatever it is that you came to do. Just wait until my son is gone, and we can handle this shit."

This big-headed muthafucka gonna laugh and reply, "Man, you dumb as fuck if you think I'm gonna kill yo' ass in broad daylight in this busy ass parking lot. I got some questions, and you the only person that can give me answers right now. You're more useful to me alive than dead."

"Trin, I can't believe after all we talked about last night that you would set me the fuck up," I said while looking over at her.

"It's not what you think. Just talk to your cousin and put all that animosity to the side for us and all we 'talked about'," Trinity replied putting emphasis on talked about.

Instead of getting out the van, she took a seat with Lenny on her lap and pointed at Montez. "Y'all need to put away the egos and lower your damn pride and remember who the hell you are to each other. Baby, if you can forgive me for what took place, then you need to forgive Montez too. We are both to blame for having that affair."

Taking what Trinity had said into consideration, I turned to face my cousin, and for the first few minutes, we sat and grilled each other before we started laughing. "I don't know what you think I can tell you or what questions you have, but before you ask them, let me assure you that I didn't kill A'Kirah nor did I have anything to do with her being up in Diamonds. I learned all that I know the night she died."

"And what exactly did you learn?" Montez questioned.

I contemplated on how much information I was willing to

tell him because if I was gonna be honest, I didn't trust his ass no further than I could throw him, and Montez wasn't small. "Look, all I can share with you right now is what she was doing in your club. I'm trying to figure everything else out, but it's not easy being in hiding. I knew that you would automatically assume that I was behind everything, so I left the city. But if you agree to a truce and allow me to get my product off without any problem, then I can get information sooner."

"That ain't gonna work. I need to know who is gunning for me," he replied.

"Can't do that, cuz. I don't think they working alone, and I'm trying to see who else is involved. If I start naming names, then you gonna take 'em out and will still have someone out to take you down."

"This was a waste of fucking time! Trinity, make sure your ass is at work tonight. I'm out!" Montez said, getting ready to exit out the van.

"Wait!" Trinity yelled, causing my son to jump in his sleep, which pissed me off. "What Stefon is saying is true, Montez. If he gives you everything he knows right now, then how can you take care of everyone? If Stefon didn't care about you, then he wouldn't have left me and his son in order to get more information. Y'all ain't just cousins; y'all are more like brothers, and shit don't have to be like this. If we didn't creep around behind his back, then none of this would be happening. At least not with you two on opposite sides of the fence. You would be working side by side. For the sake of Granny, put all the bad blood behind you and do what it takes to make sure neither of you end up dead. God forbid whoever else is involved succeeds in taking you out. Granny is getting old, and her heart won't be able to handle that shit. So, for her, if nothing else, let shit go and do what it takes to handle the enemy. But the enemy is not in this van!"

"You should've been a lawyer and not a hoe," Montez said to Trinity.

"Aye, watch your fucking mouth!" I warned him.

"What? Her argument was good, and it makes sense," he clarified.

"Baby, let Montez call me what he wants. His opinion shouldn't matter. It doesn't bother me what he thinks. Don't lose sight of what I said. This can work for everyone involved," my son's mother added.

Montez cleared his throat then spoke up. "Alright, listen, this is what we can do. I'll let you make moves without interruption as long as you're able to provide weekly updates on who I got to take care of. The minute I feel like it's no longer beneficial to me or my business, then all bets are off. I'm basically letting you eat off my plate. Do what you have to do, Stefon, to get me what I need."

"Sounds like a deal, but before you get out, let me give you my first tip. Switch up how you handle business at the club. Your shit been bugged, and your moves are being tracked. They planning on hitting the joint and taking whatever cash and valuables you have there."

"Good looking," Montez said while getting out the van and walking off.

"Baby," Trinity called out. I could pick up on the hesitation in her voice where, just moments ago, it was filled with confidence and optimism.

"You know you fucked up, but it's all good," I told her.

"But, Stefon, I did it for..." she started to say, but I cut her off midsentence without finishing.

"It's all good. No need to explain. It is what it is, and it's over and done with. Wasn't no blood shed, so we good. I just thought we were better than that and wasn't going to pull no more sneaky shit. You could've given me a heads up and explained why you felt Montez and I should sit down instead of throwing me in the lion's den unprepared." I wasn't trying to come off so harsh, but I needed Trinity to understand her place and know that moving forward, she needed to show me where her loyalty lies at.

Trinity was quiet for a second before reaching for my hand, which I gave her, "I tried that, Stefon. Many times in the past few weeks, but you weren't hearing me. If I told you Montez was meeting us here, then you wouldn't have agreed to it. This was the only thing I could think of, and I have no regrets."

"Just don't do no shit like this again, no matter what the reason behind it is. At the end of the day, we need to be transparent about everything. We have to consider the other's feelings and respect their wishes. I wasn't ready to have this sit down and squash shit with Montez just yet, but you left me no other option. You just added more to my already full plate because I have to keep his greedy ass fed with information I'm not sure I can deliver."

"I get it. I'm sorry," Trinity expressed, sounding down.

To show her I wasn't mad, just upset she took matters into her hand not knowing the dangers she placed us in, I blew her a kiss. "Aye, I'm gonna go drop this van off and then catch a Lyft back to the house. I'll meet you there. Let Tia still come over at night to stay with Lenny in case I have to make some moves. Plus, I don't want anyone to really know I'm back home fully."

I watched my girl secure our son into her car, and once she was gone, I started up the van. Before I could pull out, I got a text on my phone that Trinity had given back to me. It was a picture of me and Montez in the van talking with a bunch of question marks.

*Fuck! If it ain't one thing it's another*, I thought to myself while slamming my hand against the steering wheel. How the fuck was I gonna convince Rodney that it wasn't what it looked like? Even me looking at the picture, it looked like we were plotting and scheming, which was the case. I had to figure out some way to make Rodney believe that meeting with Montez was my idea and that I was trying to get him to squash the beef so I could bait him in. The only problem was Rodney wasn't a dumb muthafucka, and he trusted very few. One wrong move, and everything would be for nothing.

I texted him back and told him we needed to link up soon to talk face to face. Just as I was getting on the expressway,

Rodney texted back with four simple words: Don't play with me. In the time I'd been dealing with his crazy ass, I knew exactly what that statement meant. If I lost his trust, I lost my life. I couldn't shake the eerie feeling that things were about to get read bad and bloody, and my first priority was making sure none of the blood shed belonged to my girl or son.

With my phone connected to the van's Bluetooth system, I called up Trinity, and on the second ring, she answered. "You miss me already?"

"I do, but that's not why I'm calling. I want you to start looking for a new place to stay. Preferably out of the city."

"Why? You know how much money it costs to move?" she asked.

"That doesn't matter. I'll pay whatever it takes. Just do as I asked, Trin," I said.

"Okay. I'll do that when I get in the house, but I'm not looking far out." I didn't really care where she looked, as long as it wasn't within the city. Her nights working at Diamonds would be coming to a stop as well as that little housekeeping job she does. But I wasn't gonna add all that information right now. She'd find out on her own soon enough.

My next call was to Jervon, which I got no answer, so I hung up and called right back. Eventually, he picked up. "Stefon? Where have you been, and why are you blowing up my phone like you one of my bitches?"

I had to laugh at his square ass talking about multiple bitches just because he was engaged to two women. Last I heard, Fayth cancelled his ass, and he was just with one. "I know you ready to see me. Meet me at the warehouse tonight around eight."

When he didn't respond, I had to make sure I didn't lose service. "Hello?"

"I'm here. Umm, I don't have... I mean I have to... Fuck, Stefon, when you stopped responding to me, I found someone else to buy what I had. The show couldn't stop because you didn't want to showcase it anymore," he said.

"Huh?" I questioned, trying to figure out what the hell he was trying to say. "Please don't try to metaphorically explain something again, because you suck at it. I'm back, and I ain't leaving again. I had to fall off the radar for good reason. Just tell your new customer you had a change of heart, and let me know when you get more pills."

*Chapter Fifteen*

# MONTEZ

*What the fuck is up with all this traffic?* I thought to myself while I was rushing to meet Laron at the stash house. The little meeting Trinity's desperate ass made possible with my cousin went better than I had expected. I couldn't lie and pretend that what she preached about me and Stefon needing to put our heads together didn't make sense. It held a lot of truth to it, and I knew if something was to happen to either one of us, our Granny wouldn't be able to handle it. That was the one reason I let him slide when he first started selling product on my blocks.

I was hoping I got to have a few words with Laron before anyone else showed up for our weekly meeting with our top lieutenants. They handled the little people on payroll and were the only ones besides me and Laron who knew where the safe house was located. Prior to getting Trinity's text message last night, I had all intentions of letting everyone know that we would know be offering pills to our clientele, but now that I made the temporary deal with Stefon, I was gonna have to put that on the back burner.

When I arrived at the house that was off in the cut, I was relieved to only see Laron's car outside. That let me know that he was alone, and it would give me the opportunity to get his feedback before everyone else arrived. Otherwise, I was gonna have to bring his ass out into the backyard, where it would be safe to talk in private, and I didn't want to do that with how much the temps had dropped recently. I never wore those big heavy ass jackets that weighed you down, so you'd never catch my ass standing outside in the cold. The warmest piece of clothing you'd ever see on me was a hoodie, and that season been long gone.

"Whew, I'm glad you beat me here and turned the heat on. It's colder than a bitch out there," I said to Laron, stepping inside the house and closing the door behind me.

"Look what the fuck you got on. You know they design these things called coats for weather like this, right?"

"Let me ask you this. Have you ever gotten into a fight in the winter?" I questioned Laron.

"What kind of question is that?"

"Answer it."

"Of course, I have. Hell, you been right there beside me, kicking ass," Laron said.

"Okay. Now have you ever gotten into a fight any other time of the year?" I asked him.

Instead of answering me, he nodded, looking aggravated and not understanding why I was asking these questions. "So, you mean to tell me that you couldn't feel a difference in beating a muthafucka up when you have all that heavy clothing on, weighing you down? That shit prevents you from really putting hands on your opponent. I'm making sure I have an advantage over whoever I'm fucking up by not feeling constraints. But I wanted to run some things by you before anyone else arrived."

At this point, we were both sitting down next to each other, and I could see Laron processing what I had explained on why I only wore hoodies in the cold weather. "I'm listening," said Laron.

"Alright, so I been kicking it with this little bitch Fayth, and her ex is who been supplying Stefon with the pills. I've managed to use her to get him to sell me what he had, seeing as Stefon did what he's known to do, run when things get ugly," I said.

Laron started to pull at his beard then asked, "What do you know about these people?"

"Enough to where it's safe to say they green when it comes to business. I don't know how he ended up working with Stefon, but he's actually a doctor. The shit he gets his hands on is the real deal, none of those genetic brands, and I felt like I was robbing his ass when he named prices. I snatched up everything he had on him and told him to double it up next time and I'll pay him an extra five racks on top."

After a few seconds, Laron started to nod his head. "Can you trust the bitch?"

"That's a strong word. I don't trust nobody. But to answer your question about Fayth, so far, she's been keeping it a hunnid. Right now, I'm playing it day by day, but at the same time, my eyes are open and monitoring body language." I was getting ready to tell Laron about the events that unfolded this morning with Stefon when I heard a car door close outside.

I knew it wasn't anybody but Cricket and Bar, but when they entered the house, they weren't alone. With them was some tatted up white boy which caused both me and Laron to hop up with our heat aimed at our guest. "Aye, chill out, boss. He cool!" Bar shouted with his hands held up. Cricket showed his hands as well; however, the white boy stood unbothered.

"You must want to die," Laron said, taking the safety off and putting one in the chamber. "You already know how shit goes, and ain't nobody supposed to know about this spot."

"You right, but the homie cool. He got some information for y'all and wouldn't tell us. He knows who killed A'Kirah and didn't trust us with the 411," Cricket explained.

"My man, listen, I'm only coming here out of respect for the game. Let me holla at you in private," said the unwanted guest.

"Laron go pat Casper down and check him for wires. Then go see what he talking about," I said then turned toward dumb and dumber. "You better hope this shit don't come back to bite you stupid muthafuckas in the ass."

"Snow. The name's Snow," the white boy said while Laron

checked him for weapons. "And with all due respect, I'd rather speak with you and nobody else."

There was something about this man that I actually liked. He held his composure and had the same arrogant demeanor that I was known for. I contemplated on what my next move was going to be, but going with my gut instinct, I agreed to his request. "Aight, Laron. Put tweedle dee and tweedle dumb up on what I told you, but don't let them leave until I come back, because there's more to it I didn't get to tell you either."

I had Snow follow me to the back room, and when we got behind closed doors, I said, "Let me get your phone."

Without questioning my motive, he went into his pocket and handed it to me, at which point, I powered off. I didn't know this fool and wasn't going to trust he wasn't trying to record our conversation. "Time's ticking, and I have shit to handle, so tell me what you know, and if it pans out to be true, I'll be in contact with you to see to you receiving compensation."

"I ain't here for money. Like yourself, I'm big on loyalty and business. Word on the street is somebody real close to you is working with Hot Rod in taking over, and before you tell me you're already aware of who it is, trust me, you don't. It's not your little cousin. He's just a fly trapped in a web of deceit and is too blind on his own revenge to see he's being played," Snow explained.

He had me thinking, and the only person that knew the ins and outs of my business was Laron, but there was no way in hell he'd have anything to do with A'Kirah being murdered.

But who the hell else could it be? "How do I know you ain't making shit up?"

"You don't, but I'd like to think your reputation of reading folks is true, and you can see that I'm just trying to look out. What you do with the information won't affect my life in any way."

"Where did you get the info from?"

"I own my own business. I handle evictions, and I happened to overhear someone on the phone while I was boxing up their shit, basically blaming whoever was on the other end not paying the rent after she helped him get to Hot Rod and A'Kirah. Before she hung up, she yelled out a warning that caught my attention," Snow explained, and when I raised my eyebrows, waiting to hear what that last bit was, he said, "she said they better hope you don't find out what they're up to. That was almost a week ago, and around two days later, her body was found behind a dumpster with her mouth taped shut."

I allowed a few minutes to go by, just processing what Snow had just dropped on my lap, and I kept coming up blank. "Do you remember the address you were cleaning out?"

"If you give me my phone, I can pull up all the information, including the lease holders name that was evicted." I did as he requested but also watched over his shoulder to make sure he didn't do anything more than what he said he was. He hit a few buttons and went into some app that held files for his business and pulled up the contract. I couldn't believe my eyes at the details that appeared on the small screen. There was no way in hell this was for real. Very few things blew my mind, but this had to be the most shocking revelation, hands down. How to proceed moving forward with this news was the question.

"Aight. Good looking out, but I have to get back out there and get this meeting over with. I appreciate the tip." We dapped one another up, and I had to admit he was a cool ass white boy. He looked young but seemed like he had some street smarts to him. While making our way back to the front of the house, I asked, "So what made you start your own business? Like, where did the funding come from?"

"The same reason why you decided to open up one club and are in the process of opening up another one."

I looked back at him and frowned my face. How the hell did he know so damn much about me? "We have the same banker. He's my uncle," Snow clarified. I knew what he meant by that, and nothing more needed to be said.

My plug was also my banker. Nobody outside of me and Gino that knew about our business dealings. Both legal and illegal. Stefon nor Laron knew who my source was, so I knew Snow wasn't bullshitting. And now that I looked at his facial features, he did favor Gino. Gino was connected with the mob, and I was the only black man he agreed to do business with. He primarily fucked with his own kind, Italians. And they owned the whole North End of Boston. It took much convincing and even more proving to Gino that he could trust me to make us both tons of money, and to date, I had kept my word with no plans on quitting. It was Gino who advised me to start branching out and starting some legal businesses. He even put me in contact with the realtor I'd been fucking with.

"Let's get this shit over with, because I have some shit to handle. I'm sure Laron already updated you on something I'm working on. I'm putting that on hold. Stefon is back around, and I had a meeting with him today. We called a truce, for the time being, and I've given him the green light to push his product on the block. Now that's not to say I don't have my own reasoning behind making that deal, and that will come to light at a later date. Just tell y'all soldiers that I need for them to pay close attention to who he makes these moves with and find out who his customers are exactly. That is all, and be thankful that I'm letting you dumb muthafuckas leave from here today with your life. Bring somebody else back here again and you won't be so lucky!" I warned before dismissing them.

As soon as they left, I sat down and didn't miss Laron's glare. How could I, because if his eyes had lasers in them, then he would've burned a damn hole straight through my head. "What was all that about?" he questioned. "What did the white boy have for you?"

"What I already found out this morning, so it was a waste of time. Stefon ain't have shit to do with her murder, but he is working with who is to blame," I lied. I looked up from rolling my blunt and fired it up.

I took three pulls before passing it off to Laron, who looked to be deep in thought. "I know that's your cousin and all, but he's gonna have to see me."

"Nah. Stefon lives, period. Your bitch was up to no damn good and planted fucking wire taps in my club. She was gonna die no matter what." I made sure I looked at my boy when I said that. Strangely, he nodded his head in agreement. All kinds of alarms were going off in my head, and I didn't like nan one of them.

*Chapter Sixteen*

# JERVON

Man, trying to juggle three women was driving me crazy. It wasn't the sex part that was hard, because if I was being completely honest, back in my college days, I was sleeping with more than that. It was dividing up my time between each of them when they all wanted quality time spent with them. The only one who knew I couldn't give her all to me right now was the one I actually wanted to be with forever, Fayth. She held the sole key to my heart and was the only one that could get close to it.

Shawnda and Mary were both needy and demanding, but I needed the two of them to be equally satisfied, seeing as they were the ones who were providing me with bottles of pills. I was passing everything I got from Shawnda to Stefon, now that he was back in the picture. And because Mary was able to supply me with the most, I gave those to

Montez, who was requesting the larger amount and paying me more.

Out of the three, Fayth was the laid back one. She valued the time I was able to spend at the house with her and didn't nag me the way Shawnda did. Fayth was also the one that I was the most transparent with. She knew everything I had going on. Well, everything with the exception of Mary. Fayth was also the one that was benefitting from my illegal activities because all money I made got deposited directly into our joint account, and she's been loving it. No longer were the days and nights of her bitching or being frugal when it came to money. Now it seemed like it was me trying to remind her what that account was created for. A grand wedding and a nice house to raise kids in, not the latest line of fragrance, shoes, purses, and other materialistic bullshit.

Mary was the next one that I could tolerate when it came to our relationship because she was new and had no inkling I even had a baby on the way with Shawnda or was planning on spending my life with Fayth. Mary basically took over Fayth's place where the lying goes. She believed most days and nights were occupied at the hospital and office, taking care of sick people. The only difference was, this time around, I was able to cover up the lie better due to experience. I financed a new car and only drove my old one when I was seeing Mary, and I told her I started working in Providence, over an hour away. I didn't have to worry about her driving to the hospital and asking questions. I didn't have to stress whenever I went out with Fayth or Shawnda and we took my car, Mary spotting us and my cover being blown. Yes, she knew Shawnda because they worked in the same field but for different companies, but to make matters easier, they also hated one another. The chances of them sitting down for girl talk and my secret being discovered were slim to none.

Now Shawnda, she was the worst, my biggest regret, and if I could go back in time and run away from her, I would. The bigger her stomach got, the more I grew to dislike her ass. She bitched about absolutely nothing and was beyond demanding. The drive and passion I once seen in her eyes were long gone. In its place was the same controlling glare that my overbearing mother had.

Speaking of that woman, I was on my way to go see my parents because they'd been hounding me to have dinner. Fayth was working tonight and refused to come with me. Yes, she was still a bottle girl at Diamonds, and as much as I disliked it, it seemed to make her happy. And right now, with the way everything else was in my life, I needed her to be content and satisfied. But as soon as I made enough to get out the game and we got married, she could kiss that job goodbye, because no wife of mine would be walking around half naked, serving men drinks.

Walking into the restaurant, I gave my name to the host and was led to a table where both my parents were already seated. "Mother. Father," I stated, making my presence known.

"Jervon, where's Fayth?" my mother asked, looking over my shoulder to see if Fayth was walking.

"She had work. She took on an additional job part time at a nursing home to make extra money. The sooner we pay off our debts and have a hefty amount of money saved, we can finally get married and give you those grandbabies you've been asking for."

I knew it was fucked up to keep the fact they were already about to have a grandchild, but telling them about Shawnda would mean having to reveal trouble between me and Fayth. I also couldn't tell them the truth behind Fayth's night job. Lucky for me, my father wasn't into strip clubs, so I never had to worry about him discovering my secret.

"Well, I sure wish you two hardheaded fools would agree to let us help and pay for the wedding. Just because her mother is against your relationship and won't pay for anything shouldn't mean the two of you do it alone," my mother whined.

I had just arrived and hadn't even ordered yet, and I was ready to go. Any other time I came to dinner with my folks, Fayth would be here, keeping my mother entertained. Me living a secret life was easy to do in comparison to pretending I liked this lady. She wasn't who my father pictured himself spending his life with, but her family's financial status persuaded him into picking her. He never admitted that little bit of information to me during one of our many father-son chats growing up. I happened to overhear an argument between them one night, and he blurted it out.

Enough about them and this damn dinner that I was already over. I raised my hand to get the waiter's attention, to order myself a strong drink, because I was gonna need it. I heard an all too familiar laughed and prayed I was hearing shit. Looking in the direction of the sound, I knew my night was gonna really end bad. Sitting three tables to our right sat Shawnda with I am assuming was her father. I knew if I didn't find a way to get the hell from here now, then my parents were about to find out about what I've been hiding from them.

I slipped my hand into my pockets and made my phone go off by pressing the volume button 'til I felt it vibrate then turned the ring tone back on. "I have to get this. It's Fayth, and she said she wasn't feeling well before she left for work," I lied, holding my phone in my hand.

Once outside, I took a few minutes before calling my father. "Dad, I have to go. Fayth feels lightheaded, and since her accident, she's afraid to get behind the wheel. I'm gonna have to reschedule. Tell Ma I love her."

"I understand, son, and tell Fayth I hope she feels well. Drive safe, Jervon," he replied.

Whew, that was a close call. One that I thought I managed to get away from, but I should've known I hadn't. As I was pulling out of the parking lot, Shawnda called. "Hello?" I answered.

"Where did you go? I'm here at the same restaurant you was just at, and when I spotted you, I excused myself from dinner so I could go over and say hello, but you were gone and never came back inside," she whined. Man, the squeakiness of her voice that I didn't seem to mind before now, felt like fingernails going across a chalkboard.

"An emergency came up, and I had to go. What time will you be home? I'll meet you there."

"Ah, babe, I really wanted to meet your parents and for you to meet my father." I didn't have to be in Shawnda's face to know that she was pouting, but she'd get over it later when I laid this dick on her.

"It will happen. Let me focus on driving. Go enjoy your meal," I said, hoping she would get the hint and hang up, which she did.

Deciding to go watch my girl at work, I headed to Diamonds. I probably should've used the time to go and spend time with Mary, seeing as Shawnda was spending time with her father and Fayth was at work, but I wasn't in the mood to be around nobody but Fayth. Walking inside of the club, I automatically started to walk in the direction of the VIP section you would always find me and Ron, but tonight, it was already occupied. I'd never been here on a Wednesday and figured it wouldn't be as crowded, but from where I was standing, it looked like there were more men in business suits than you would see on during the weekend.

After I found a table as close to the VIP area as possible, I sat back and waved over a server to order a drink and have her bring me some single dollar bills. I looked over to the section Fayth was working, and I knew my girl was walking out tonight with a good amount of money in tips. The way the men were lusting over her body had me feeling both mad yet proud. That was all mine, and I loved it.

I felt what made Fayth stand out above the rest of the bottle girls was the innocence in her face. She blushed whenever she got a compliment, and it showed. She didn't have the same pretty girl conceited attitude like the other girls. Even the men that were getting lap dancers from the actual strippers couldn't keep their eyes on the topless female directly in their face. Instead, they kept glancing at the beautiful masterpiece that was there only to serve drinks.

"What brings you in tonight?" Montez asked, taking a seat at the table.

"Boredom."

"Man, you one lucky muthafucka, Jervon. You know that, don't you?"

I followed his eyes, and they were roaming Fayth's curves. She must've felt someone staring at her because she looked over to where we were seated and bit her bottom lip before giving her attention back to her customer. I felt myself brick up and couldn't wait to slide inside of her later in the night. "She deserves the world."

"You looking rough these days. Everything okay?" Montez asked, still eye-fucking my bitch and not bothering to look at me while talking. I found it to be disrespectful, but I was in no position to say anything.

"Business wise, everything is great. Personal life is a whole different subject. I just want to make enough money as quickly as possible so I can disappear with Fayth. You have no idea what I have to go through to get you and Stefon product, and it's wearing me down. I'm working sometimes ten-hour days at the clinic, then I have to balance my time between women. Fayth been complaining about me losing weight and been telling me to take time off and go on a trip."

I wasn't sure why I was pouring all this out to a man I barely knew, one who clearly wanted to fuck my girl, but I didn't have anyone else to speak with, and I was pretty sure he could understand how hard it was balancing work, a drug business, and multiple women. "Will your job give you time off? If so, take your woman and get away for a week. It'll do the two of you some good. Head up to Canada and lock yourselves in a cabin or some corny shit like that."

That wasn't a bad idea, and I'd love nothing more than to shut the outside world off and spend it cuddled up with Fayth. "I'll look into it, but getting that woman to do anything spur of the moment ain't easy. The last trip we took was only for a weekend, and I had to damn near kidnap her. Actually, your cousin was responsible for that. He knew someone with a vacation house down in Florida, and I got it for free for the weekend."

Montez sat up in his seat, now placing all his attention on me. "Where did you say you went again?"

"Florida. He said it was a family member house that is rented out as an Airbnb."

"Interesting. Well, I have to get back to work. Drinks on the house, and let me know what your girl says about the two of you taking off so I can get someone to cover her shifts. Oh, and remember, our business transactions stay between us. My cousin is not to be aware of me working with you. You don't tell him shit, and I won't let him know that you just fed me some information about who he been working with to take me down." And with nothing else said between us, Montez got up and walked off in the direction of his office.

What the fuck did I get myself caught up in?

*Chapter Seventeen*

# TRINITY

Now that there was some peace between Stefon and Montez, life had become easy for me. I no longer was working during the day at the motel, and the only nights I went to the club to dance was when Fayth was working so we could spend some time together. Not that we got to sit down and catch up on everything that was going on in our lives.

I was currently lying on a massage table, experiencing what might be one of the greatest feelings I'd ever felt. The way this man was making my body feel was indescribable. I couldn't recall a time I'd ever felt so relaxed. It was as if I was floating my way up to heaven to say hello to all my loved ones that left. Some people were born with a craft that they were destined to share and never discover what that may be, but there no doubt in my mind that this man was made to do this job.

There wasn't a part of my body that he didn't free the built-up tension. Well, except for my pussy. That hoe was betraying me, and Stefon for that matter, who paid for this trip to the spa, by getting so wet I knew there was a little trail of fluid forming a puddle between my thighs. This man was exploring my outer body, but the inner parts were silently begging for the same treatment. His hands were callous free, large, soft, and gentle. Have you ever climaxed without having actual sex or foreplay for that matter?

My phone started to ring, but there was no way I was going to stop this fine ass man and the magical high he was giving me to see who it was. I knew my time was almost up, and whoever it was could wait 'til then. "Are you sure you don't have to get that? I can stop," the masseuse said.

"Don't stop." I moaned out, causing him to chuckle. I didn't care how I sounded. I was pretty sure he got this same reaction from each of his customers.

"Music to my ears. It means I'm doing my job and making you feel good."

Oh no he didn't! "Indeed, you are," I replied, flipping over onto my back. "I think my upper thigh is still a little tense."

Wasn't shit wrong with me. I just wanted him to work the imaginary kink while I watched. "Well let me get that for you. Can you give my hands some leeway by spreading your legs open a tad bit?"

"I thought you'd never ask," I flirted while doing as he asked. Luckily for the two of us, I had just gotten waxed two days ago. As his hands worked their way upwards until they were inches away from the forbidden area, I watched the bulge in his pants grow.

"Your natural scent is addictive," he complimented while licking his lips.

I knew I had to do something and fast, or else I was going to be begging this stranger to use his third leg to massage my inner walls. As if on cue, my phone started to ring for the fourth time, and that let me know that whoever was trying to reach me was important. "As much as I hate to cut this short, I think I should get dressed and see who is calling me."

"Very well." This fine ass muthafucka knew what he was doing. Looking me right in the eye, he helped me sit up with one hand, and with his other, he adjusted his very obvious hard dick. I couldn't resist as I licked my lips.

"Please come back again." He didn't have to tell me that. I already had my mind set on doing so. "I'll leave you to get dressed. We have complimentary wipes over there."

I was grateful because Lord knows I needed them to freshen up my disloyal pussy. Whoever interrupted my appointment better had a good reason. Like their legs got amputated. As I walked out the serene spa with a little zip in my step, I retrieved my phone from my handbag and saw it was Fayth calling me, which was alarming. My girl wasn't the kind of person to blow up someone's line, so something had to have happened during her trip to Canada. I was happy for my friend. It seemed like things were falling back into place for her finally. Jervon seemed like he got his shit together. At the same time, she gained some independence and was living for herself.

"You sure have bad timing and know how to fuck up a good time," I said into the receiver as soon as Fayth answered. When I didn't hear anything, I got alarmed. "Fayth?"

"I'm here." She sniffled.

"What he does and where he at?" I asked, automatically assuming that Jervon fucked up after I just gave him some credit.

But like the saying goes, you only make an ass out of yourself when you assume something. "Nothing. Are you busy? Do you think you can go with me to the clinic?"

"I was in the middle of something but just left. Where do you want to meet up?" I asked without questioning why she needed to be seen. It really didn't matter. I liked Fayth, and like myself, she didn't really get along with females, so she had no friends.

"I'm at home. I couldn't even make it into my day job. I feel like I'm dying. The whole vacation was a waste because I spent it in bed or hovering over the toilet seat."

"Ah, did you take a pregnancy test?" I asked while getting into my car and fastening my seat belt.

"No. I think I just ate something bad," Fayth replied. If she wanted to believe that bullshit, then I'd let her think I believed her, but we both knew that wasn't the case. Eating bad food would either run its course within forty-eight hours or send you to the emergency room. Judging from what Fayth was telling me, I knew her diagnosis all too well. Her ass was pregnant.

It took me about forty minutes to reach Fayth, seeing as the spa I went to was all the way in Waltham. When she walked out the front door of her building, she looked worse than she sounded on phone. Her eyes were bloodshot red and puffy. Her skin was so pale she almost looked like she bleached her skin. Don't let me start on the rat's nest that sat on the top of her head. I poked out my bottom lip to let her know I sympathized with her.

I didn't even ask her what clinic she wanted to go to; I just headed in the direction of the obstetrician I used when I was pregnant with Lenny. They did free pregnancy testing between the hours of four and six. "Where are we going, Trinity? I look like hell and really don't want anyone to see me like this."

"We going to the doctor," I answered her.

"But my clinic is in Hyde Park."

"Fayth, face it. You about to be a mother. I'm not even the one who spent years going to medical school, and I already know what's wrong with you. There ain't no need to sit up in some clinic, or emergency room for that matter, and get tons of tests done when you can take one simple test."

"And what if it's not that? Then it's wasted time," she said.

I didn't bother to respond as I pulled into the parking lot and parked. "If the test shows negative, you can rub it in my face that I was wrong, and I'll pay for a late lunch."

Reluctantly, Fayth got out the car and followed me inside.

2

The good thing about getting the free test done, they didn't ask for insurance information or any of that. They simply had you write your name on a list and handed you a cup to piss in with your name written on it in marker. They took it to the back, and within ten minutes, someone was calling you to a small room to go over the results. Once Fayth did all but the last step, she took a seat next to me, and I could see the nervousness kick in. Her leg bouncing was a dead giveaway.

"Fayth?" Nurse Loretta called out. I loved her out of all the nurses here, and I was glad it was her handling Fayth's test because she was the best.

Fayth looked at me, and I stood up and reached for her hand. "Come on. I'll go in with you."

"Thank you," she replied softly.

Together, we stepped into the small room, and me and Nurse Loretta shared hellos while I introduced her to Fayth. A minute later, I was handing my friend some tissue after hearing what I already knew. It was positive. Nurse Loretta asked Fayth some standard questions and provided her with pamphlets with everything she needed to know about moving forward with the pregnancy or terminating it. She encouraged Fayth to not make any decision now, and lucky for her, according to her HCG level, she was just over four weeks, so she had time to decide.

The second we got back in my car, Fayth broke down and kept saying more to herself than to me, that she couldn't have the baby, although she didn't believe in abortions. Knowing my girl needed me, I reached over and consoled her. "If you don't believe in them, why are you even considering having one?"

She sat back up and faced straight ahead and replied, "Because I don't know for certain who the father is. If I was a little further, then I'd know for certain it was Montez, but me and Jervon started back having sex about a month ago."

I guess I understood where she was coming from. What woman wanted to play a guessing game on who fathered her child? But what surprised me was the fact Montez was even a contender. In all the years I'd known him, and even during our own little affair, I never knew of him to sleep with someone without a condom. I didn't want to pry and ask her intimate details pertaining to their sex life, so I left it alone.

"Fayth, don't go making decisions based solely on that. And don't take what I'm about to say the wrong way, but in my opinion, I don't think you should even mention to Montez he could be the father. Just tell Jervon it's his and keep it pushing. He's more grounded and is a better fit to raise a baby. Yes, Montez treated Lenny good whenever he was around him, but at the end of the day, it wasn't because we were sleeping together. It was because that's his little cousin and he loves him. But Montez has way too much shit with him and is in deep in the street."

"I hear you, but I don't think I can lie about something so serious. What if one day my baby needs blood or something, and Jervon finds out he isn't the father? I can't do something like that. I'd rather lay all the cards on the table, and when I give birth—if I follow through with this pregnancy, that is—then we do a DNA and find out."

I pulled out of the parking lot and started driving back toward Fayth's house. "Fayth, I'm only telling you this because I like you, and you are a little naïve but in a good way. Montez is a user. He don't give a fuck about anybody but himself, and when a person is no longer beneficial to him, they get disposed. I've talked bitches off ledges behind his ass, while they had him on the phone, pouring their heart out. He would tell them women to jump and hang up. He's not who he is pretending to be. That man ain't ready to be anyone's daddy, and it wouldn't be fair to your baby to have someone who thinks tossing some money your way will cover his responsibilities. Jervon, on the other hand, I can see attending parent-teacher conferences, ballet recitals, football games..."

"I'm scared. I don't know what the hell to do, and my head is starting to hurt. I'm gonna go home and lay down. I'll figure everything out another day."

*Chapter Eighteen*

# FAYTH

Not being close to my mother was really hitting me with what I was dealing with right now. I could really use her advice on what to do, but how would I reach out and explain everything to her without her judging me? There was no way I could tell her I wasn't sure who got me pregnant without having to tell her everything, including Jervon cheating. It was bad enough I turned my back on her and ignored her warnings on the kind of man he really was.

I was currently sitting in the middle of my bed with all the pamphlets that Nurse Loretta had handed me three days ago. I was trying to figure out who was the father. She mentioned I was about a month pregnant, according to the HCG levels found in my urine. I leaned over and grabbed my phone to pull up the calendar, and that was when I realized Montez was more than likely the father. How I didn't realize weeks ago I missed my cycle until now, I couldn't answer, but sure enough, according to what my eyes were seeing, I should've gotten my period the same night I slept with Jervon again.

This shit was starting to give me a headache. What were the chances that it could actually be Jervon's? I mean, was it safe to say he wasn't a candidate, or could I have conceived the same day I was supposed to get my period? I may be wrong, but if I remembered when we covered this in class, I shouldn't have been still ovulating so close to when my period was due. In order for me to be certain, I knew the best way to answer any questions was making an appointment and seeing what the doctor said.

One thing I was able to decide on was going through with the pregnancy. I called and hung up the phone over a dozen times while attempting to make an appointment to terminate, but every time the phone rang, my heart sank. It was God's plan for me to conceive, so I was having my baby, regardless of who went half with me in creating it. Who was I to question His actions?

Another thing that kept running through my mind was how good it would feel to have a little person to love me unconditionally, no matter what. That was all I'd ever wanted, and I thought I had that with Jervon for years, until he proved otherwise. I wouldn't have to worry about my child going out and cheating on me. I was sure there would be times when they get older that they would lie, sneak, and even hurt me, but that was a part of life, and I'd be ready to deal with that.

I was so deep in thought that I didn't hear Jervon come in the front door, and it wasn't until he was already in the room did I realize he was here. It was too late to hide the papers that were spread out on the bed, so my secret was out the bag. "Wait, does this mean what I think it does?" he asked.

Not able to find the words to answer him, I simply nodded my head, letting him know that yes, I was with child. He instantly got excited. So much so that he began to cry. He pulled me up onto my feet and started to hug me so tight before pulling away and placing his hand on my stomach.

"Fayth, baby, please don't kill my baby. I know you wanted to be married before you brought a life into this world, and that can still happen. We can elope and just have a big wedding later on, if that's something you still want. I'll do whatever you ask of me if you keep our baby. I love you so much, and you're the only woman I want. You're the only one who I love, and if you agree to keeping the baby, I'll spend the rest of my life proving it to you." Jervon pleaded, but what he didn't know was my mind was already made up, and even more so, this may not even be his baby.

I was shocked at him suggesting we run off and get married. I didn't know how to feel about that. My mind kept going back to the speech Trinity gave me in the car about Montez and how he would be an absentee parent if he were to be the father. I knew from all that Jervon was saying and the steps he wanted us to take together before I gave birth that he would probably be the better option. But I had no say on whose genes my child would carry. "I'm not getting an abortion, Jervon. But I don't know about getting married either. We still have so much to fix within our relationship, and a baby shouldn't be the reason we rush marriage."

"Why do I sense something's wrong, Fayth?" he asked.

*Because there's no guarantee the baby belongs to you,* I said to myself, although I wanted to speak it out loud. Just that fact alone, I knew I couldn't marry him. Not until I knew who got me pregnant. Even if I had to sneak and do a test behind his back without his knowledge. Then and only then would I agree to become his wife. That was if he wasn't married beforehand. I think he kept forgetting that he had a pregnant fiancée across town. One that would be giving birth long before I did.

"How do you plan on this working out when you have another woman thinking you belong to her? One who happens to also be pregnant by you, Jervon. We may not bring it up when we are together, but we also can't ignore the fact that she's pregnant by you."

Jervon became quiet for a few minutes. "You're right, Fayth, and it's time I man up to my bullshit and stop stringing Shawnda along. I'm gonna sit her down and come clean with her. She deserves to know that my heart is here with you, and if her baby turns out to be mine, I'm gonna be a man about it and take care of my responsibilities. Stefon and Montez are gonna have to understand that I can no longer supply them with pills. I'm choosing you and our future. I'm putting you first."

All of what he was saying warmed my heart, but it was too

late for all that. Trust was a funny thing, and once broken, it could never go back to how it once was. It was like knocking a pretty vase off a shelf and a corner piece broke off. You buy gorilla glue and put the pieces back together, but when you looked closely, the crack would always be there to remind you that it was broken. This outside child that Jervon was having with this woman would be a constant reminder that the trust I once had for him was broken.

Never mind if it turned out that Montez was the father of this baby how Jervon would feel knowing I never told him I slept with another man. As far as he knew, he was the only man I'd been with. I wanted to tell him right now, but I also knew telling him without talking with Montez first wasn't wise, because the second Jervon found out I'd been sleeping with Montez, then the little business they'd been conducting would stop. But how was I supposed to talk to Montez about it without revealing to him that I was pregnant?

"I appreciate all of what you're saying, Jervon, but with the way things are right now, it wouldn't feel right getting married. I know I always said I never wanted a child out of wedlock, but I can't get married just because I'm pregnant."

"I'm gonna fix this. I know I've been saying this for weeks now, but I mean it. I'm gonna go right now and tell Shawnda that I'm moving out."

"Don't. Not yet. She is pregnant, Jervon, and you owe it to her to be by her side while she carries your child. Breaking up with her while she is this far along can cause the baby to go into distress if she starts stressing. It's important for a mother to remain as calm as possible for the health of her unborn child. If something were to happen due to you leaving her pregnant, it would bother me. I can't have that on my heart, not to mention, karma is a bitch," I told him.

"What about our baby and this pregnancy?" he asked.

"I'll be okay. I'm aware of your situation, and I won't allow it to stress me out. Once she gives birth, we can revisit this conversation, but for right now, my mind is made up, and I stand by what I just said."

"You're perfect! You know that, don't you, Fayth?"

All I could do was nod my head. Little did he know, I mainly said all of that to buy myself more time. I needed to speak with Montez and let him know everything. I know that if I told Jervon that Montez may have fathered my baby, then he would stop providing him with the pills. In the meantime, I'm gonna encourage Jervon stay with Shawnda.

For the next few hours, we relaxed in the bed, watching movies and eating saltine crackers. Once he left to return to Shawnda's house, I got up and showered. I was going to Diamonds to have this talk with Montez because the sooner I got it over with, the sooner I could fully relax and begin to enjoy this blessing growing inside of me.

When I got to the club, Bully, the bouncer that worked the door, gave me a hug like always. "Where's boss man?" I asked, playing it off like I was another employee and not someone Montez was fucking.

"Not here yet, but he should be arriving soon. You working tonight?" Bully asked.

"Nah. Just had something I had to talk to him about. I'll go hang around inside and help out if needed." We said our goodbyes, and I walked inside.

I could see why Montez wasn't here clocking the dancers' moves, because it wasn't busy at all. The girls that were working were the clubs least favorites, and the only reason they made any kind of money was if the few like Trinity were tied up with other customers. Taking a seat at the bar, I said, "Wow, it's dead in here tonight."

"Tell me about it, girl. I don't know what happened, but like an hour ago, three girls walked out. I called Montez, and he said he would take care of it. I ain't heard back from his ass since. As soon as they left, two of the VIP's cleared out too," Linda, the bartender said, filling me in on the tea.

I wonder what could've happened to make three dancers quit. It couldn't be because they were all fucking Montez and found out. Even I knew, as someone he slept with, that he did nothing in secrecy. If he lets one of the girls service his needs, then that was just what it was. I didn't know all of that until I started working here and listened in on them talking in the back. The crazy part was many of the girls hated me because I was being labeled as his favorite. Whatever that shit meant. Trinity advised me not to pay too much mind to them, and it was best if I was sleeping with Montez still to keep them out of our business. They would run to Jervon in a heartbeat to tell him with hopes of fucking up things for me.

After an hour passed and still no call back from Montez, I tried him one more time and got his voicemail. I gave it another twenty minutes and dialed his number again but got the same result. He must have been kissing someone's ass to get them to come back to work for him, and just thinking about that pissed me off. The only reason I was caught back up with Jervon was because Montez asked me, and I was beginning to feel played.

One more attempt to call with no answer, I decided to leave a voicemail. "Look, I came to the club to tell you in person that I'm pregnant. I'm keeping my baby, and before you say anything, I don't know who the father is. I'm gonna live my life, and you live yours. I won't bother you, but I would like for us to take a test so I can know for certain if it's yours. Jervon wants for us to get married, and I'm gonna let him sign the birth certificate."

The second I left that message, I instantly regretted it. I didn't know why I was being juvenile, but I couldn't help but to think that what Trinity said in the car was true. Montez was using me as his little puppet to get what he wanted from Jervon, and I fell into his trap. Now I was sitting here pregnant and confused on who the daddy was.

## Chapter Nineteen

# STEFON

*Earlier that same day*

I didn't know what the hell I was thinking by telling Trinity to find a house that she could see herself living in for the next few years until we were in the position to buy our first home. Here we were, walking up the pathway to look at the sixth house of today alone. Never mind the fact we'd been doing this for the last three weekends, and Trinity found something wrong with every listing.

"I think this one might be it," said Trinity while she knocked on the door.

"You said that about the last two we looked at today. Just wait 'til you see the inside before you speak," I replied. I didn't mean to sound uninterested, but how hard was it to find someplace to move into. Everything we'd looked at was better than where we were living at currently.

I shifted my sleeping son from one arm to the other, when finally, the door opened. The rental agent that stood there was fine as hell, but I knew if Trinity saw me checking her out, she'd automatically turn the house down, and I was ready to get something to eat. "Welcome. Feel free to walk through and view the house. It's been recently renovated, and I must tell you that if I didn't already own my house, I'd move here in a heartbeat. The owner spent a good amount of money on the details. It's three bedrooms, two baths, full size washer and dryer in the basement, which also has been renovated. The rental price is two thousand seven hundred eighty-five dollars a month, with nothing included but maintenance."

God must've heard my prayers, because after Trinity inspected the house, she finally found something she liked. We filled out the rental application and left a security deposit equivalent to one month's rent behind.

"Oh my God. That house was so pretty. Don't you think so, Stefon?" Trinity asked on way back into the city.

"I think you're pretty," I said, complimenting her, and like always, she blushed.

"I'm serious."

"So am I," I said. I could feel her smile start to fade, and I didn't want to ruin her mood, so I added, "Relax, Trin, baby. I like the house, and I can't wait until everything goes through and we get the fuck out of Boston. I can see myself playing with Lenny in the yard, building snowmen and shit."

I couldn't actually picture that because I hated the damn snow, but I knew it was something I would be out there doing regardless, making memories with my son. "I'm hungry for some curry chicken. What about you?" Trinity asked.

"You read my mind because I was gonna stop off at Flames and grab something to eat, but we gonna have to go through McDonald's and get Lenny some nuggets or something."

This was how life was supposed to always be for us, and looking in from the outside, one would never think that months ago, we weren't even speaking. But the power of love, when it was real, was a force that nothing and no one could break, and the bond me and Trinity shared was Teflon strong.

I left Trinity and my son in the car and went into Flames on Blue Hill Avenue to order our food. While inside, my phone rang, and without looking, I answered. "Talk to me."

"Nah, you talk to me. What you got for me?" Montez asked.

Making a deal with this impatient muthafucka was something I was beginning to regret, even if he was my cousin. Granted, being able to move around and make money without any repercussions was cool, but the stipulations behind it sucked. "Nothing. But I am making rounds in a little bit and gonna see if I can find anything out. This time, I'm not calling ahead and just showing up, hoping I can stumble on something to give you."

"You better hope so, because the clock is ticking, and my patience is starting to wear thin." And without another word, he hung up. I swear if it wasn't for my granny, his ass would be dead.

I placed an order for two plates of curry chicken with

brown rice, peas, and cabbage, and took a seat while they made the plates. Ten minutes later, I was back in the car and driving home deep in thought. Thankfully, Trinity was busy chatting on the phone with who I guessed was Fayth, and I couldn't help but hear the words baby and abortion come out of her mouth. I knew damn well if she was talking about her being pregnant, she wasn't considering killing my seed. She must've felt me looking at her and shook her head to let me know she wasn't talking about her.

Back at the house, I dug right into my plate, while Trinity got Lenny situated in his seat with his nuggets and fries. "Cup," he said, looking at me, and unlike when I first came back home, I knew exactly what he was talking about. Not to mention, we'd been taking time out of our schedule to help him speak clear. I got up and filled his sippy with his favorite Juicy Juice berry flavored juice and sat back down.

"Aye, so check it out. I have to run out to make some moves and check on some things. I shouldn't be gone too long, and when I get back, I want us to sit down and talk about the future. Seeing as we're gonna be moving and starting fresh, I want everything to be new. I'm not talking about just the furniture in the house either. Anything from our past—all dirt we've both done will be left here. Nothing but positive vibes moving forward," I said.

"I've already disposed of that trash, Stefon. I'm all the way in, baby." Hearing her say that let me know that everything I'd been doing was worth it. At first, Rodney wanted me to come back under false pretenses and use my son's mother to get information on Montez. But I couldn't do that. The love I have for Trinity was the real deal. Crazy how Montez flipped shit around, and here I was trying to find out more on what Rodney had going on.

I got up and tossed my plate in the trash and leaned down to give my girl a kiss before kissing my son then left. The sooner I left, the quicker I could be back where I wanted to be. The sun had just gone down, and as I made my way up Rodney's street, I noticed a car that was all too familiar in his driveway. Parking a little ways down, I noticed the door to his house cracked, and the thug in me automatically reached for my gun and removed the safety.

Just as I was getting ready to get out my car and make sure Rodney was good, I spotted Laron stepping onto the porch. My first thought was someone was talking, and word got to Laron that Rodney was who killed A'Kirah, and Laron was here to avenge her death, but what I saw next blew my fucking mind. Rodney stepped onto the porch with him, laughing. The two embraced in a brotherly hug before giving each other dap. I wish I was able to make out what they were talking about, but I really didn't need to know. Instead of pulling my trigger, I snapped a few pictures with my phone and waited until Laron left.

I knew if I just went to Montez and told him that his right-hand man was a snake, he wouldn't believe me. He'd call bullshit and would renege on our agreement. That was something I couldn't afford now that I was getting ready to move my family someplace that cost twice as much as where we currently laid our heads. But one thing about pictures was they didn't lie. Now, had Laron and Rodney been at a standstill, then Laron could easily lie his way out of why he was here to begin with, but it was clear to see he didn't have any issues with Rodney.

The second the coast was clear, I started my car and drove off. I thought I saw someone standing in the window of Rodney's house, but I couldn't be sure, and I wasn't going to let that stop me from rushing to my cousin and show him my discovery. I couldn't help but to think that with what I had in my possession, I would be able to keep pushing pills on Montez's block and not owe him anything in return.

On the way to Diamonds, which was where I knew I would find Montez, I couldn't help but to wonder why Laron would be cool with Rodney killing A'Kirah. He must not know that she died at the hands of the man he just hugged. There was no way and Rodney would be left breathing. Unless of course Laron was trying to bait him in and get him comfortable enough to strike.

Five minutes away from Diamonds, I spotted a large police presence up ahead. It looked as if they had a car pulled over and were searching it with K-9's. The closer I got, I started to make out what kind of car it was, and when I realized it was Montez the police had hemmed up, I froze. At first, he wasn't in custody, but when I saw the dog go crazy at the rear of Montez' car and saw the officer reach for his handcuffs, I knew the dog hit on something. That wasn't like Montez because he never drove around with work on him.

Laron was the one who typically transported the drugs from one place to the other.

Driving forward so I could get to my auntie's house and have her call the lawyer Montez had on retainer for things like this, I passed the unmarked car as the detective was putting Montez inside. Our eyes locked and he mouthed the words, "you're a dead man walking."

Chills went up my spine, and I couldn't believe my cousin thought I was capable of being a snitch. No matter what bad blood we had between us, he was still family, and even if he wasn't, a rat was something I would never be. I shook my head and proceeded to my auntie's house. But things got worse when I saw her house surrounded with even more police. Whoever was behind setting Montez up was close enough to know everything he owned was in my auntie's name. That let me know it wasn't a random stop but that they had a search warrant. Someone was talking, and I had a good idea who it was.

Not knowing who the hell to call to help out my cousin, I decided to go back home. When I got to the door and put my key in, I realized it wasn't locked. Rushing inside, my heart sank to my feet. This can't be life right now. How the fuck did they find out where Trinity lived? But more importantly, where were my girl and son?

"Welcome home, my love! It's sad I had to track you down at this disloyal hoe's house!"

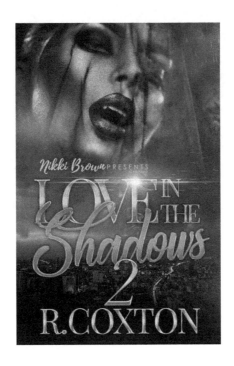

**AVAILABLE 12/13**

# CHRISTMAS WITH NBP

## Available Starting 12/10

CPSIA information can be obtained
at www.ICGtesting.com
Printed in the USA
LVHW050813210820
663741LV00013B/1244